Hazardous

Kings of the East #13

Charity Parkerson

Punk & Sissy Publications

Copyright

—Warning: This book is intended for readers over the age of 18. Some of my books contain allusions to past abuse and trauma. I try to have nothing triggering on page and treat every situation with care.

$\mathcal{C}ontents$

Author Note   1

Introduction   2

Chapter One   5

Chapter Two   18

Chapter Three   49

Chapter Four   76

Chapter Five   85

Chapter Six   115

Chapter Seven   135

Chapter Eight   164

About the Author   178

Content   180

Author Note

THIS SERIES IS DARKER than my usual writing. If you need a list of potential triggers, you can skip to the end of this book and find a list after the About Author page. You can also visit my website at charityparkerson.com/kings-of -the-east, if you'd prefer.

Introduction

WULF AND BEAU HAVE** **nothing in common. There's no reason for them to see each other at all. So why can't they stay away?

Wulf's friend married Beau's brother. That's it. They have no other common ground. Wulf isn't certain they even like each other. They have nothing to talk about when Wulf finds himself on Beau's couch. Neither of them calls or sends texts between unexpected visits. At least, not any calls or texts that matter. Wulf thinks they might be in a relationship, but neither of them has talked about it. Since Wulf works for a crime family and Beau has met most of them, he needs to figure this out. He's never been good with words.

Ever since Wulf showed up at his door, distraught, several months back, Beau has been finding little gifts on his porch like a cat brings dead birds. Wulf is a little dark and a lot scary. He's also intense and fascinating. Beau hasn't been interested in anyone else since they met. He's terrified to ask if they're a couple because he has a bad feeling Wulf is a criminal. Ignorance is bliss, except Beau thinks he might also be in love with Wulf, and there's a good chance Wulf is extremely hazardous for his health. Everything about them is a mess.

Hazardous is the thirteenth book in Charity Parkerson's Kings of the East series where assassins, crime lords, and mafia bosses run the world. These books are best when read in order.

Chapter One

THE KNIFE'S HANDLE BIT into Wulf's palm as hc waitcd. His grip tightened by the second with impatience. The sound of footsteps approached, and he shifted slightly, slipping deeper into the shadows. The muggy Florida heat had sweat rolling down his back. His shirt molded to his skin. Wulf was used to the discomfort. He couldn't let it deter him from his task. Just as Wulf suspected he would, as Beau stepped onto the hidden porch, he had his head down and his gaze locked on his keys. Beau possessed zero sense of self-preservation. Today, it would be his downfall.

Wulf lunged. He pressed his knife to Beau's throat. "That's how easy it would be. If I were anyone else, you'd be dead. When do you plan to listen to me about these ridiculous vines surrounding your porch? They're nice, but they hide your door from sight. I could be anyone. I could've broken into your house, and no one would've seen." He leaned his weight into Beau, grinding his crotch against Beau's ass. "I could've been a rapist."

"It's good to see you too, Wulf."

He sounded so calm, as if men held knives to his throat every day. Wulf decided he could be the same. "How was your day?"

"Hot and dirty. Do you want to come inside and shower with me?"

Wulf spun the knife away from Beau's skin and sheathed it. "Yeah, okay." He couldn't be sure, but Wulf thought he caught Beau hiding a smile as he let Wulf inside. This was their routine. Wulf's only real friends were his teammates, Dante and Jericho. Dante had married Beau's older brother, Marshall. The move had basically left Beau and Wulf to keep each other company, since Marshall had been the only person Beau ever spent time with and Jericho never spent time with Wulf outside of work. Most days, Wulf wasn't sure if Beau even liked him. He definitely had no clue if they were dating, but Wulf didn't want anyone else. If Beau touched anyone else, Wulf would kill them, so here they were, in some weird sort of stage of together yet not. Wulf wasn't exactly sure how they had gotten to this point. Dante had gotten hurt on the job. Wulf had stopped by to let Beau know he wouldn't see Marshall for a while because of that. Beau had invited him in and cooked him breakfast. Breakfast had become lunch, and then it had been breakfast time again before Wulf had known what happened, and then Wulf had kept coming back for more ever since.

Cool air washed over him as they stepped inside. Wulf watched as Beau emptied his pockets on the table by the door. He had a lot of trash in his pockets from working all day. Tiny plastic twist ties and plastic bits from whatever he did at his brother's pool cleaning business. Wulf knew Beau was the manager there, but Beau also spent most of his day out on job sites. While Beau emptied his pockets, Wulf separated the important stuff from the trash. If he didn't do it, Beau would let it pile up, and that bugged Wulf. Wulf was a biohazard specialist. He cleaned crime scenes. Technically, he also killed people and cleaned up after other people who killed people, so he was pretty fucking invested in things being spotless. Beau wasn't the same. Despite cleaning pools all day, he was perfectly okay with leaving a mess for his cleaning lady. Messes were evidence. Every piece of trash told a story. Wulf couldn't let Beau leave a mess behind. He toed off his shoes by the door and carried the bits of plastic to the trash can.

As he tossed the pieces inside, Beau pressed against his back. "That's how easy it would be. While you're distracted by my trash, I could pounce and take advantage of you."

A smile snapped to Wulf's lips. That was why he kept coming back. Wulf never smiled before Beau. Beau was just genuinely a nice guy. He was a normal person who didn't know about all the ugliness in the world. Beau made Wulf feel like he could live a regular life. He could come home to Beau every night, have dinner, watch TV, and go to bed. They could make love and fall asleep in each other arms without Beau ever knowing Wulf was exactly that: a wolf.

"Take advantage of me, then." Even Wulf heard how breathless he sounded.

"I'd rather pamper you. Come take that shower with me. Then I'll make you dinner and you can rub my butt."

It was all so goddamn ridiculous. Wulf shouldn't care about this guy. Beau was ten years older than him and—honestly—he cared a bit too much about money. Wulf imagined that stemmed from a childhood of going without nice things. None of that shit bothered Wulf. Age was only a number, and he had all the money they would ever need. He could also rub Beau's butt for as long as he wanted.

"I like this plan." He really did. Wulf couldn't wait to do that shit all night.

Beau had no damn clue why Wulf kept coming around. He was about ninety-five percent sure they were in a relationship, but that other five percent kept him up at night. Wulf had money—like a fuck-ton of money. Money that someone his age—with no family and a job as a biohazard specialist—didn't come by legally, but goddamn, he was hot, like super model hot. He had this shaggy brown, curly hair that was always in his whiskey-colored eyes and a full torso-sized tattoo that just screamed "bad boy." Fuck, he made Beau ache. Likely, Wulf would just disappear one day and never look back. Until then, Beau intended to get as much of Wulf as possible.

Just thinking about how Wulf looked beneath his clothes had Beau's dick stirring. Rather than leading Wulf to the bathroom, as he had planned, Beau's hand automatically snaked down Wulf's body. Before he reached Wulf's crotch, Wulf spun and shoved Beau against the wall. Beau's mouth went dry. Sometimes, being with Wulf was like unleashing a monster. He had something dark inside him. Beau liked to fuck it. He was kinky like that. Beau was a little surprised Wulf hadn't figured that out yet. Just like with Wulf pulling that knife on him earlier. That had turned him on way more than it should have. He had known there was no real danger. Beau didn't want to get hurt for real, but he liked to play. For too many years, Beau had filled an empty space inside himself with nameless sex. Then Wulf had come along, and damn, Beau didn't feel quite so hollow anymore.

Wulf's mouth covered his and a loud moan escaped Beau. He wouldn't have called it back even if he could. Wulf was never rough with him. In fact, he always took Beau to bed like a proper gentleman. Beau wanted to get fucked like a dirty whore. His jeans loosened. Beau's fingertips dug into Wulf's arms. He kissed Wulf deeper, desperate for what he offered. Their shirts disappeared and their mouths clashed. Beau's cock leaked. There was a swamp of pre-cum inside his underwear. His mouth found the top of Wulf's tattoo on his shoulder. He licked. The taste of salt filled his mouth. It was obvious Wulf had been outside, sweating all day. He practically tasted like the sunshine. Beau moved lower, tracing the line of the tattoo down the seam of his arm until he counted each rib with his tongue. Beau dropped to his knees and unbuttoned Wulf's jeans. His gaze flipped upward as he set Wulf's erection free. Beau's breath caught at the way Wulf stared down at him. There was so much pent-up passion inside Wulf. Beau didn't know how to convince him to unleash it. For someone so dark and dangerous, he never let go with Beau.

Beau licked Wulf's dick from root to tip, then swallowed him. Wulf made a sound that had Beau smiling inside. Beau had tricks. He could twist Wulf into knots. Wulf wouldn't know what hit him. Even as Beau sucked, he continued stealing Wulf's pants, so he could play with Wulf's balls. He wanted quick results this first time because he had no plans of letting Wulf come. Beau was proving his worth, so maybe Wulf would be real with him finally. Wulf was safe here. Beau needed him to know it. He needed Wulf to see that Beau saw the real him. That was why Beau set a pace meant to please. He bobbed fast on Wulf's dick, letting saliva run down his dick, wetting his shaft and balls. The sounds Wulf made let Beau know he did a good job. Beau sucked and pumped faster until he felt Wulf's muscles tense. Right when he felt that first twitch, Beau squeezed Wulf's cock, cutting off his orgasm before it happened. A pained cry escaped Wulf.

Wulf slapped his palms against the wall above Beau's head and left them there. He didn't move or make another sound. It was almost terrifying how still he went. Beau watched and waited. Wulf stared straight ahead at the wall. He didn't as much as drop his chin to look at Beau. It was odd. Beau had never gotten this reaction to orgasm denial. When Wulf's breathing returned to normal, Beau started again. He went right back to sucking Wulf's dick like nothing happened. Because Beau did this all the time, he knew—when Wulf came—he would experience what felt like multiple orgasms at once. Beau would get his reward later. After they showered and Wulf got his strength back, this huge cock would make Beau feel like he was torn in two. He couldn't wait. Beau fought the urge to jack off just thinking about it. Fuck. Before he met Wulf, he had only had toys as big as Wulf. Damn. Wulf made Beau feel like a wanton. He was, but wow. Beau was addicted.

He felt Wulf tense again. Beau put his heart into blowing Beau this time.

He wouldn't stop. Wulf openly fucked his mouth, even as he tried not to hurt Beau. He never touched Beau's hair like most men would. He kept his hands on the wall. All the abuse Beau took was self-inflicted. Suddenly, Wulf ripped away from him. Hot cum hit his face.

Wulf immediately panicked. "Shit. I'm sorry. Don't move. I tried to pull out quick enough I didn't hit you with it."

Beau fought a sigh. He had been ready to swallow. Wulf was already wiping the cum away with his discarded t-shirt, as if it was poison on Beau's skin. Beau couldn't be upset about it. Wulf was fucking perfect. He was rich, respectful, and caring. Absolutely flawless. It was sweet enough to rot his teeth. Honestly, Beau thought he might be in love.

Chapter Two

THE HOT FLORIDA SUN beat down on Beau as he skimmed leaves from his fifth pool of the day. He lifted the hem of his shirt and wiped sweat from his brow, flexing his abs in a show for the men lounging nearby. The Wright twins had been paying Beau's brother's company to clean their pool for three years now. Beau exclusively did the job. Sick, tired, or hurt, Beau never missed this appointment. They were his favorite clients.

"You know the drill, sexy. A hundred dollars more an hour exclusively to you when you do the job shirtless."

He always made them say the words. No freebies. They weren't the only clients that paid more to see Beau's body. Marshall didn't know that part. He kept that bit strictly under the table. Beau looked the twins' way and winked before he peeled his shirt up and over his head. He tossed it aside.

"Mhmm. That's better. You look hot today. Do you need a drink?" Hale made the offer, sounding every bit like a devil luring him to his doom.

Beau had made that mistake more than a dozen times. Hardy and Hale were a very good time. They had money and no shame. But until Beau knew for sure if he was in a relationship, he didn't want to fuck things up with Wulf. Beau had a good thing going with Wulf. "No, thank you. Not today. I still have a ton of stops."

Hale pouted. "You've been telling us no for months. Are you bored with us?"

Hardy ran his hand down Hale's tan chest until he cupped his junk. "Do we need to lure you inside with the story of our first night together?"

Beau didn't want to be turned on by that, but they were sexy and—goddamn. They would do things. Things no moral, normal person would do. He had seen shit in this house. Things he wouldn't forget. Beau shook his head, trying to shake off the growing lust. He had a man at home. Beau would not ruin that by playing with the twins today.

"It's not you. I really don't have time these days. Marshall got married and his husband is basically the same age as his daughter, and hot, so fucking hot."

"Ooooh," both twins cooed simultaneously.

He knew he had them then.

"There's no getting him to come to work
these days."

"Fair," Hardy said, going back to sipping
his drink as if pacified by Beau's excuse.

Beau went back to work. He made good
money at this job. Way better than most,
he imagined. That was because he had
always been willing to play with his
clients like the Wright twins for the right
price. People had ideas and fantasies
about their pool boys. As a pansexu-
al guy who was also kinky as hell and
had zero self-respect, he was here for it.
Something had changed since meeting
Wulf. Beau just couldn't explain what,
because Wulf was not kinky. Not at all.
Not even a little. In fact, Beau had never
been with someone so respectful. It was

odd. He thought no one would tie him down, much less some guy who liked to cuddle and didn't spank him at all. Beau couldn't figure it out. He had something with Wulf, though. Beau wouldn't fuck it up by being self-destructive if he could help it. Not just yet, anyhow. It was possible they were doomed.

Beau made it through the twins' appointment and the rest of his stops while somehow still making the same high tips as usual, with Wulf owning all his thoughts. By the time he made it home, he was more than ready for a shower. As he headed for his front door, he eyed the bushes and vines Wulf hated so much. They were climbing vines that hid the entire porch and front door from view. He loved them. Beau felt like he lived in a hobbit's hole. He had no intention of ruining his dream home to make Wulf more comfortable. Not only had he paid a fortune to a specialty landscape artist to have them designed, he enjoyed the constant lectures and never knowing when he would find Wulf's knife against his throat. Beau shivered at the thought. That had been much hotter than he cared to admit. Beau doubted Wulf wanted to hear that. He didn't find Wulf waiting today. Beau didn't have time to be disappointed. In Wulf's place, there was a box. A smile immediately exploded across Beau's face. Wulf was always leaving weird little gifts like a cat left dead mice. Beau never knew what he would find next.

He carried the box in the house while holding his breath. When it came to Wulf, Beau knew the gift could be anything. Wulf was a little weird and endearing like that. The container wasn't heavy. That didn't really mean anything. In the few months since Wulf had been turning up at his door, Beau had found all manner of things waiting for him. Heart-shaped rocks, a gold necklace, diamond earrings, a pretty crystal fish, a bag of marbles, and countless other things that made little to no sense had sat waiting on his porch. Even if Beau had no idea if he would be floored or confused, he couldn't wait to see what was inside. Beau toed off his shoes and headed for the couch. He sat and ripped open the box. As he popped open the lid, a gasp escaped. It was a jeweled crown. Beau had no idea if the stones were real, but it was fucking beautiful. His hands shook as he lifted it from the box and the jewels caught the light. They shimmered. Beau had always liked shiny things. He blew out a breath. Damn. He really would fight anyone who tried taking Wulf from him. Maybe Wulf was like some crazy wild animal Beau was trying to slowly tame, but fuck. He had Beau mesmerized.

An idea struck. He put the crown back in the box and jumped from the couch. Beau rushed into the bedroom and grabbed some clean clothes. He would take a shower and then head to Wulf's place. If he wasn't home, then maybe it was Beau's turn to hide in the bushes. He was crazy over Wulf, and it was time he showed it. It was damn sure way past the time he found out if they were a couple. Tonight felt like the night. He needed to know where they stood.

Jericho, Dante, and Wulf had been a team for years. They were like brothers. In fact, they had the same last name:

Wrath. If anyone asked, they said they were cousins, but truthfully, Wrath was the name of their team. The three of them had chosen their profession, but they had been handpicked by Zander to work together and he had been oh-so right to put them together. At least, for Wulf's sake. If not for any other reason than for this day.

Every six months, the three of them reported to Corey's to get their bi-annual STI results. For most people, it might not be a big deal. Hell, it probably didn't matter to Jericho or Dante, but they showed up for Wulf. Even though all three of them had been sold into various sex worker positions as children, Wulf's childhood had been a hundred times worse than most. Each time these tests came back negative, it was another six months he had survived. His team showed up to have Wulf's back in case this was the time those tests results changed, even though—logically—Wulf knew they likely wouldn't after all these years. Sometimes, logic had nothing to do with anything.

His foot tapped, and he chewed the side of his nail. No one looked at him. Wulf appreciated that more than anyone knew. Dante swept his long hair up and twisted it into a bun before securing it with a band on his wrist. Jericho's light blue eyes stayed locked on the door, waiting for Corey. No one said a word. Corey, or Dr. A., as some people called him, treated all the kids rescued from Zander's efforts to eradicate child sex trafficking. Wulf couldn't imagine the mental toll Corey took, but then again, they all were barely hanging on most days. Part of Corey's home had been transformed into a medical wing. It was as clinical as any hospital, but still the three of them sat together like three parentless kids, waiting for judgment in the principal's office.

The door finally opened, and Corey swept inside. As always, his white doctor's coat looked impeccable and his brown hair was perfectly brushed, as if he needed to have control of one thing in his life. With his gaze locked on his laptop, he blindly snagged his rolling stool and moved their way.

"I have everyone's test results. Even though we go through this every six months, you know the drill. I still need everyone to state out loud that you give me permission to share your test results with everyone present."

"You have my permission," they chanted simultaneously.

Corey nodded. "Going in alphabetical order, Dante, everything came back negative. No abnormalities. Jericho, everything came back negative, except for one inconclusive. I think it was contaminated, though. Let's run that one again before you leave. Even if it comes back positive this time, it's something minor that can be cleared with an antibiotic, but like I said, I don't think it will be. It's rare for that one to be positive after coming up inconclusive first, but I'd like to run it again just to be sure."

Wulf thought he might have a stroke. His heart pounded in his ears. It never took this long to get to him. It was like things were purposely being drawn out to torture him.

Jericho made a dismissive motion. "That's cool. I can stick around to retake the test. Read Wulf's results."

Corey nodded and went back to clicking on the laptop. "Wulf, everything is negative. No abnormalities."

Jericho touched his knee. It was barely a brush. Most people wouldn't have noticed. Wulf saw it for the show of support it was. Jericho knew exactly how much relief poured through Wulf's veins at Corey's words. He had six more months. Wulf had been handed another half a year of freedom from consequences of the actions of others. He didn't have to feel guilty for continuing things with Beau.

Wulf's phone rang before he had a chance to thank anyone for showing up for him. His eyebrows snapped together in confusion at the sight of Ransom's name. He quickly answered.

"Hello?" He looked the guys' way and pointed at the phone, letting them know it was important. They nodded, and he headed outside.

"Hey, Wulf. It's Ransom. We got a silent alarm at your house. So I checked the footage and a guy just came through the front door. I wanted to run it by you before we went in. Do you want me to send you a still shot of his face, or should we just send in one of the guys?"

Wulf didn't hesitate. He couldn't think of a single person who would break into his home, but he definitely wanted to see who they were. "Yes." His phone shook and Wulf checked the device. He snorted without thought and pressed the phone to his ear again. "Disregard the alarm. That's my man. He must've accidentally set off the alarm."

"Okay. That's why I always check. I'll let the guys know just in case this happens again."

"Thanks, Ransom. I appreciate it. Talk to you later."

"Sure thing."

As Wulf disconnected the call, Jericho stepped outside. "Is everything okay?"

Jericho was the calm one. The soft-spoken one. He was the one who appeared to have adjusted to normalcy in a way Wulf never would.

Wulf nodded. "There was a false alarm on my security system, but I'm still going to head home and check it out. What about you? Do you need to talk or anything?" He wouldn't elaborate. Corey hadn't made an abnormality sound like a horrible thing, and Jericho didn't look freaked out. He already had a cotton ball taped to his forearm and his keys in his hand. But if Jericho needed someone to talk to, Wulf would stay to listen.

Jericho shook his head. "I'm not worried. You know me. I live like a monk." Jericho flashed a tight smile as he made the claim and Wulf couldn't tell if he was joking or not. Honestly, Wulf did not—in fact—know Jericho like that. For all Jericho's willingness to listen to other people's problems, he never confided in other people. Jericho was like still waters. He gave the appearance of living like a monk, but—for all Wulf knew, Jericho had a harem at home.

Wulf couldn't make him talk about it. "What about Dante? Is he sticking around and hanging out?"

"He plans to stay and hang out for a little while. I think Marshall is on his way so they can have some couples' night or whatever."

That was definitely Wulf's cue to leave. Marshall didn't know yet that his younger brother had been seeing Wulf. Wulf didn't know if there would ever be a reason to tell him. He still didn't feel comfortable around Marshall. It wasn't Marshall's fault. Wulf was very much like a wild animal. He didn't take to most humans. Wulf needed to leave.

"Yeah... I'm out."

A knowing chuckle followed on Wulf's heels. "He still doesn't know about Beau, huh?"

Wulf stumbled. He hadn't known Jericho knew about Beau. Wulf glanced behind him. "Uh. No."

"Why? You two have been together since Dante was shot, right? That was like..." Jericho stared into space for a moment, obviously calculating time. "Eight months ago."

They were parked next to each other. It wasn't like Wulf could hide. He had to face this and... damn. It had been eight months. They were a couple. He was dating Beau. Like for real, for real dating. Most couples had already exchanged "I love yous" and house keys by now. They hadn't even put a label on themselves. Jesus.

Wulf forced himself to focus on the topic at hand. "I don't know why we haven't told Marshall. We're just taking things slow, I guess. Probably because we haven't even established if we're dating." Wulf blew out a sigh. "You know I'm fucked up, man. I'm trying. That's something, right?"

Jericho smiled. It was the small smile a parent gives when they see a child making strides. That was Jericho in a nutshell. The adult of their group. "I'm proud of you. Marshall is a great guy.

I'm sure his brother is too. Whenever you get around to talking about it, I'm sure Beau will be just as amazing as Marshall was with Dante when he found out what Dante does for a living."

"I'm sure." The words popped from Wulf without Wulf even having to think. He had given Beau hell when they first met. After all, Beau was a typical, single, sexy gay who knew his worth. That was what Wulf had hated about him on sight, because Wulf had never gotten to be him. It was jealousy. Then Beau had shown him kindness at his lowest and now Wulf couldn't stop going back like the stray he was.

Jericho nodded and dipped inside his X7, freeing Wulf from his thoughts. Wulf jumped into his Gladiator and fired it to life. He didn't care about anything but getting to Beau. It was strange that Beau had broken into his house.

They should talk. It was time. Wulf took several slow breaths. He could be human. Just because he had been raised like an animal didn't mean he was one. He could do this. Wulf would go inside, sit down, and tell Beau how he felt. He would ensure Beau understood he wanted only him. Wulf had this.

He pulled into the garage, killed the engine, and took another steadying breath. They were a couple. Always had been. There was no reason to be nervous over a simple conversation. Wulf stepped out of the vehicle and headed inside. He stopped dead in his tracks the moment he stepped inside. Beau waited for him at the door, wearing nothing but the crown Wulf had left for him. The intricate piece looked every bit as gorgeous on Beau as Wulf had known it would.

"Goddamn."

Beau blushed.

Wulf swallowed. His gaze slid down Beau's nude body. Wulf forgot what he planned to say. His feet moved. He didn't know if he shut the door. It didn't matter. Nothing mattered but Beau. Wulf crossed the room and swept Beau from his feet.

"My king."

Beau held on to his crown and laughed as Wulf ran for the bedroom. He gently set Beau on the bed like the treasure Beau was before tearing off his own clothes like the desperate fool he was. Wulf ripped open the bedside table and found the lube. Beau's laughter was the only thing that kept Wulf from feeling like an idiot. He had never wanted anyone as badly. It wasn't until Wulf had a condom in place, the bare minimum of lube, and Beau's knees in the air that a hint of sanity returned, but it was too late. A loud moan tore through the air as Wulf pushed his way inside Beau's asshole. Their gazes collided. Hazel eyes filled with desire called to Wulf, making him human again.

Wulf's shoulders relaxed. He took a breath. Then another. Wulf lowered his head and whisked his lips across Beau's, slowing things down. Beau deserved a man who made love to him—like the king he was. Wulf pulled out a hair and thrust, rocking against him. Their lips met and clung. They shared air. Their breaths were labored as they strained toward the same goal.

"I've been thinking."

Beau chuckled and then moaned as Wulf thrust at the perfect angle. Wulf couldn't let Beau's mind clear too much as he made his confessions.

"I realized today we've been doing this for eight months."

Beau's fingernails scored Wulf's skin, making him hiss. "Not this exact thing. This is the first time you've made love to me while I'm wearing a crown."

"To me, you're always a king."

At his confession, Beau cupped his face and pulled him in for a deep kiss. For a moment, Wulf lost himself. It felt too good inside Beau. His body kept trying to suck Wulf deeper. He had never been more enamored by anyone. Beau made a sound around his tongue that made Wulf forget what he meant to say.

Beau tore his mouth away and grabbed hold of the headboard. He strained against Wulf, visibly fighting for the orgasm he wanted. He was the sexiest man Wulf had ever seen. It didn't matter he was nearly ten years older than

Wulf. Men Wulf's age were weak compared to Beau. Beau had confidence to go with his beauty. He knew his worth. Beau knew he deserved his crown. Wulf couldn't look away from Beau's face. He was fascinated by the way he owned his pleasure. Beau made Wulf want to please him.

Then Beau met his stare, and the world went silent. Everything else disappeared. Beau looked incredibly serious for someone on the verge of orgasm. "Yes. We are dating. I've been yours since we met. Stop questioning yourself."

Something inside Wulf broke. It was as if Beau had reached inside his head and read his mind. He swore they were connected at that moment. It was as if Beau knew him and accepted him. Wulf did something he never did. He rolled to his back, giving Beau control. A hint of shock crossed Beau's features. For a moment, Beau sat on his cock, staring down at him like he didn't know what to do. Then, Beau let him know he made the only good choice in his life when he had chosen Beau. Beau moved his crown from where it had fallen on the mattress and hung it on the bedpost. And then he made love to Wulf. There was no other way to describe it. He held Wulf and rocked himself on Wulf's cock. Beau lingered over Wulf's lips, mesmerizing Wulf with tantalizing kisses. The day passed with them joined together. Beau took his time. Every time Wulf came close to orgasm, Beau changed directions and tempo, or stopped altogether, stealing the moment. Yet Wulf had no complaints. He had never felt closer to anyone.

Finally, Beau settled onto his feet and bounced on Wulf's cock. With his head thrown back, he gave Wulf a show, stroking himself while riding Wulf's dick at the perfect angle. Just when Wulf didn't think he would make it until Beau came, cum shot through the air and coated his skin. Beau's cries mixed with Wulf's as Wulf fought to get deeper inside Beau. The only time he felt whole and right was when they were together. He wouldn't lose this. Beau wouldn't regret him. One way or another, Wulf would make him happy. They would make a good couple.

Beau didn't want to move. He knew they should probably find something to eat or do anything at all other than play footsie and kiss, but Beau was happy. When Wulf first showed up in his life, he hadn't known what to expect, but it hadn't been this.

"I feel a little dumb."

Wulf's quietly spoken confession made Beau smile for no reason at all. "Why?"

"I don't know why I was scared to ask if we were a couple. Maybe I was afraid you'd say no and then stop seeing me. I don't know. It's just me, I guess. I'm pretty good at screwing things up. You're the one thing in my life I never want to ruin."

"Why?"

Wulf's sexy whiskey gaze moved his way. "What do you mean, why?"

A coy smile tugged at Beau's lips. "Come on. We've refused to acknowledge we're dating for eight months. Let's not stop there. Lord knows, we might not have this talk again for another year. Why are you afraid of losing me?"

Wulf stared at him for so long, Beau didn't think he would answer. Finally, he smiled, looking like a shy kid, and reminding him of their age difference for the first time. Wulf usually seemed older because he was too serious. "I care about you."

"Just care?" Beau didn't know why he couldn't stop pushing or teasing. He had never seen this side of Wulf. Beau liked it.

Wulf shrugged. A blush touched his cheeks. That hint of embarrassment broke Beau. Beau never expected it from Wulf.

If Wulf couldn't expose his heart, Beau would. If Beau wasn't good at anything else, he was excellent at being a fool. "It would break my heart if I never saw you again. I'm very much in love with you, Wulf Wrath. I'm more than afraid to lose you. It terrifies me."

Wulf took a ragged-sounding breath. His gaze never wavered from Beau. "It's a good thing you're settling for smaller tips from the kinky twins, then."

A loud huff escaped Beau before he could stop. "I see you've been stalking me again today." He rolled onto his back, ready to leave the bed and find something to eat. It was obvious Wulf wasn't ready for this serious of a conversation. He didn't care that Wulf followed him sometimes. If that was what Wulf needed to feel secure in their relationship, then whatever. Beau was a little crazy too. He couldn't judge. Before he could move away, Beau found himself pinned to the bed by Wulf's weight. He looked like the wild animal he had been named after.

HAZARDOUS

"Where are you going?"

Beau didn't answer.

Wulf stroked his hair. His gaze moved over Beau's face. He looked hungry. "I was only teasing. You never have to worry about money as long as you're with me, but I will kill those boys if they touch you." A shiver ran down Beau's spine at the darkness in Wulf's tone, but his cock stirred. Wulf meant it and the warning turned Beau on way more than it should.

"Why do you care if they touch me?" He knew he was taunting at this point, but Wulf hadn't returned his words. Not only that, but he had also practically accused Beau of prostitution. Maybe he borderline had done that in the past, but that wasn't Wulf's business. Like everyone, Beau survived.

Wulf stroked Beau's bottom lip. He followed the motion with his gaze as if he already pictured his cock there. "Because I love you more than I love myself. I don't care enough about what happens to me to let anyone else touch you." Wulf's gaze moved back to hold Beau's stare, and Beau knew. Wulf meant every word. He was dangerous. Beau had never been more aroused in his life... or in love. He should be terrified.

Chapter Three

RUTHLESSLY, WULF WALKED THE scene and put a bullet in every head. Each body had already been checked for pulses, but Wulf didn't take chances anymore. Not after almost losing Dante. They had shown up for a simple clean-up eight months ago. Three men. They were supposed to be dead. Wulf had checked for a pulse on each one and felt nothing. But when Dante had gone to take care of the first body, the guy had popped up and shot him. Never again. Now, Wulf took zero chances with his team.

Dante sighed. "You know you're making an unnecessary mess, right? It's been eight months."

Wulf put his gun away. He would never let the lecture bother him as long as everyone went home safely. "I'll gladly scrub an extra hour so you can go home to Marshall."

With a shake of his head, Dante moved to take care of the two bodies farthest away, leaving Wulf behind. Wulf glanced Jericho's way and eased in that direction, trying not to look like he made a beeline for him.

"Hey."

Jericho glanced up from his work. "Hey."

"I talked to Beau last night."

"How did that go?"

Wulf nodded unnecessarily. "Good. We established we are dating."

"Good." Jericho went back to working.

Wulf didn't move. "Is it okay if I talk to you about something awkward and uncomfortable?"

Jericho didn't look up from his task. "We're elbow deep in the entrails of perverts, so really there's no better time than now."

That was what Wulf thought, too. Their gear and the gruesome scene made any talk of their past or emotions seem less traumatic somehow.

He jumped in to help Jericho and talked while they worked. "Like I said, we talked, and I understand we're dating now, which seems dumb now that I look back on it, but you know me."

"I do."

Wulf didn't take that as an insult. They were being open and honest. Wulf was a mess. They both knew it. "Despite it being me, I feel pretty good about how things went. He told me he loves me."

Jericho's head shot up. Their gazes met through their hazmat helmets. Jericho wore a huge grin. "Did he really? That's great."

Wulf nodded, and they went back to work. "It was nice. I said it back, which really shocked me. Honestly, I kind of rode a high for a few hours last night. Then he went to sleep, and I got to thinking."

"Uh oh."

Yeah. Jericho knew him. Wulf didn't let that slow him. "I'm kind of boring."

Jericho laughed. "You just shot six dead dudes in the head."

Wulf shrugged. "No, really. I'm not that exciting. There's been several times I've gotten a vibe from Beau that maybe he's a little wilder... in the bedroom than I am." Wulf felt uncomfortable as hell, but he knew he could talk to Jericho about anything. Jericho was just that guy. Nothing ruffled him.

"Okay."

Jericho's bland tone kept Wulf talking. "You know where I came from. I had a hard enough time accepting I was gay in the first place after everything that had been done to me. For a long time, I never wanted another person to touch me at all, much less a man. In fact, the first time I had sex with another man willingly, I threw up afterward. I just... I don't know. I don't know if I can handle being what he might need long term, you know? If he wants anything from me beyond the bland, my mind might come completely unglued and I don't want him to see that."

Jericho nodded. "That's not surprising." He seemed to think it over for a second before blowing out a sigh. "Why do you think Zander put the three of us together as a team?" Jericho didn't wait for Wulf to answer, which was a good thing, since Wulf had no idea where this was going. "Do you think it's a coincidence that we're gay? He rescues hundreds, if not thousands, of kids a year. Yet the dozens of us that are gay always end up together in the same towns, bonded for life. That's no accident, dude. Zander knows we'll need each other for moments just like this." Jericho took a breath. His chest expanded and then caved as he released the breath. "Look, lots of guys have kinks. Some of them are small. Others are sick. I seriously doubt you went into dating this guy without digging into every aspect of his life. If you didn't find any real dirt on him, then I'm sure his kinks are harmless ones. It sounds like he probably just wants some role play shit. If you like him and want to be with him, lean into it a little and see if you can take it. If not, then be honest. Really, either way, you need to be real with the guy. Tell him you have a rough past, and you don't know much your mental health can handle, but you like him and you're willing to try. You are willing to try, right?"

Wulf nodded. "I'll admit, it's getting a little harder to compete with the kinky twins every day."

Jericho laughed. "I have no idea what that means."

"You might be better off not knowing."

"No way," Jericho said, tossing chemical onto a blood trail. "You have my curiosity up now. Distract me from our current hell with a lurid tale."

Wulf laughed and fell into the story of Hardy and Hale, who were the bane of Wulf's existence. Jericho was right. Wulf had investigated and stalked every inch of Beau's life. He had uncovered every dark secret that could be found. What he had found was Beau liked money and had way more green than anyone knew about. His savings was fat. That discovery had led Wulf down a rabbit hole, following a trail of rich, high-tipping customers. People loved their pool boys, especially when they were shirtless and liked to play. Even more especially when they were between them—like Hardy and Hale. Beau hadn't touched them since he started dating Wulf. Of that, Wulf was certain, but Hardy and Hale touched each other. A lot. For a lot of money. It turned out twin porn was a very popular genre in the business, and the pair were raking in the dough. Wulf honestly didn't care what they did, but he had meant what he told Beau. He would kill them if they touched his man. Some things were sacred. Their relationship was one of those things. Wulf wouldn't lose Beau. He had nothing else.

There was another box waiting when Beau got home. Beau bit his bottom lip at the sight of it. He didn't want to smile like an idiot, but the package was brightly wrapped with a yellow bow. Normally, when Wulf left gifts for him, they were haphazardly wrapped in random paper, or they were in a box that might have come from anywhere. This was a whole new ballgame. The only other time Beau had found a present this carefully wrapped had been on his birthday. That was when he had gotten the diamond earrings. Beau had gotten his ears pierced again just to wear them. His ears had been pierced as a teen, but they had since grown in, and he had to get them redone. Beau had been more than willing for the gorgeous two-carat diamond earrings. Now he had to know what warranted another beautifully wrapped gift. With Wulf, the surprises never ended.

Beau headed inside while nearly dancing with excitement. He barely made inside the door before he ripped off the ribbon. When he lifted the lid, tears filled his eyes before he realized it would happen. There was a house key with a small heart-shaped key chain on top of a folded note.

With a sniff, Beau pulled out the key and unfolded the note. He blindly set the box on the sideboard as he read.

Please come and go as you want. My alarm code is 3460. I had to tell my alarm company not to have you arrested yesterday... even though it might have been kind of hot to see you in handcuffs.

Love you,

Wulf

Beau drew a steadying breath and pressed his hand to his stomach as the butterflies stirred. He read the words again. Beau owned some handcuffs. He could grab them and plan a date.

"That's the first time I've seen you smile like that."

A scream tore from Beau. The letter flew into the air. Beau's heart pounded in his chest as he scrambled for safety with nowhere to go. Wulf smiled unrepentantly from the couch. Beau bent at the waist and tried to catch his breath. It had been a long time since anyone had scared him as badly. Beau found the note and key where they had gone flying before he straightened. He set them on the sideboard and emptied his pockets while still trying to get his heart rate under control. Beau would be damned if he let anyone see him weak. Part of him wanted to be mad, but he had used a YouTube video to pick the lock on Wulf's front door, so he couldn't complain. With his pockets empty, Beau opened the drawer on the table and grabbed a spare set of keys he kept for his house. He still couldn't look Wulf's way again. His temper wasn't quite under control.

"I didn't mean to scare you."

Beau jumped again as Wulf molded against his back and did his usual gathering of the trash from Beau's change and keys pile. A smile tugged at Beau's lips as he watched the ritual. It was such a small thing, but that tiny show of care made Beau wonder how Wulf hadn't known Beau loved everything about him. How could he not?

Beau turned in Wulf's arms before he got away. He held up the key to his house. "It's only fair. You shouldn't have to break in either."

Wulf took the key and tucked it into his front pocket. He kissed Beau's cheek. "Take your shower or whatever you need. We have plans."

Beau's eyebrows rose. "We do?"

Wulf nodded.

Beau loved surprises. Wulf had been full of them lately. "Okay. Give me like fifteen minutes."

Wulf stole a deep kiss before stroking Beau's ass. "Take your time. I'm not going anywhere."

With his bottom lip held between his teeth, Beau hurried into his bedroom to get showered and changed. Wulf had always been unpredictable, but lately, he had been downright shocking. Beau rushed through, getting ready. He couldn't wait to see what Wulf had planned. Wulf waited patiently for him, as promised. As soon as Beau was ready to go, he led Beau outside to his Gladiator and opened the passenger side door for him. A gorgeous red rose waited on the seat. Beau shook his head and smiled. "You're amazing." He climbed inside and brought the rose to his nose. Beau waited until Wulf was behind the wheel before he asked what he really wanted to know. "Why are you always buying me gifts? You know you don't have to, right? I don't expect it."

"I know." Wulf shrugged, looking uncomfortable. "I don't know why I do it. Things just remind me of you, and I can't stop myself. Like you're soft and smell good like a rose. That bag of marbles is another good example. I was working one night, and I stopped by this small corner market to grab something to drink. The marbles were on the counter, and they were the exact color of your eyes, and it was like I had to give them to you. I don't know why I'm this way."

Beau leaned his way and linked his fingers through Wulf's. "You're perfect. Don't overthink it." He would never want Wulf to change. The fact that he was so unique was how Wulf had won

Beau. Wulf was like settling into a fairy-tale. One where he won the beast.

They drove around aimlessly until darkness fell and Beau's curiosity was through the roof. Wulf maneuvered down a back country road not any vehicle would have traversed. When they came to a rundown shack in the middle of the woods, Wulf parked. The clouds parted, and the moonlight shone brightly on the hollowed-out building. Beau eyed the place. He wasn't sure if it was meant to be their destination or if Wulf had just picked a place to stop. He didn't imagine anyone would come to this spot unless they knew it existed.

Wulf ran his hand around the steering wheel, looking uncomfortable. "After you told me you loved me and fell asleep last night, it kind of hit me. You don't really know me. Not where I come from or my past."

Beau tore his gaze away from the shack and focused on Wulf. Wulf's tone put him on high alert. Beau immediately made a dismissive motion, trying to stop Wulf before he started down this road. "I fell in love with the man who shows up every night, holds my hand, takes care of me, rubs my butt, and falls asleep beside me. It doesn't take a genius to see." Beau stopped because he didn't want to offend Wulf. He tried a different tactic. "I can tell you probably didn't have the greatest childhood. I've never brought it up because I don't need you to cleave yourself in two to let me in or whatever. If you need me to love you just as you are now and never tell me where you started, I can and will live with that. I don't need you to bleed for me to prove yourself."

Wulf nodded, but never looked away from the house. "I know. That's one of the many reasons I love you, but we do have to talk about it at least a little, because I think I'm failing you."

Beau's heart dropped. He had no idea Wulf felt like that. "I never meant to make you feel that way."

Wulf glanced his way. He looked wrecked. Beau wanted to beg him to stop this. Wulf shook his head. "I know. It's not your fault. There's nothing wrong with you. It's me. You're completely normal. It's that I'm—" Wulf growled, sounding frustrated. "Come on." He stepped out of the vehicle.

Beau followed because he had to know what he had done wrong. He had thought they were fine. Wulf waited. When Beau reached his side, Wulf took his hand and headed toward the house. As they got closer, Beau realized it was burned out. At some point, it had been set on fire and the backside was collapsed. Wulf circled the building until they came to what looked to be an old fire pit and doghouse with thick chains attached. To Beau, it looked like a place where huge backyard parties had once been held. Likely, bored teens still used the place on the weekends to get drunk and make out.

Wulf made a halfhearted gesture. "I was rescued from here when I was eleven." Before Beau recovered from the blow, Wulf pointed at the doghouse. "They kept me chained there. The guys who owned this place, they would host these weekend-long parties where they would invite all their redneck trucker buddies. They would get high and pass me around between the guys. No one slept, especially me. If I wanted to eat and not get tortured too badly, I did what I had to do."

Never in his life had Beau hurt as badly for another person. Tears filled his eyes. His chest hurt and he couldn't breathe. He didn't dare make a sound or let a single tear fall. The crazed look in Wulf's eyes said it all. If Beau fell apart, he would never see Wulf again. He showed Beau a part of himself no one had ever seen. How Beau reacted now would make or break them.

"I didn't bring you here because I wanted you to know this about me. Fuck, I never want anyone to know any of this about me. Yesterday, I did my bi-annual STI testing, and I thought I would fucking lose my shit. Like my mental health is complete fucking bullshit. Some days I'm barely hanging on. Everything came back negative, by the way. It always does. But the thing is, you're not like me. You're not fucked up. Sometimes, I can feel the way you want to go farther than I'm willing and I think I'm holding you back." Wulf met Beau's stare and Beau realized something monumental. He really did love Wulf. It wasn't just words. They were building something together, and that meant building on a foundation of a past that might not be that mentally stable. Beau was okay with that.

"What are you holding me back from?"

Wulf shrugged. "I honestly don't know, but I know you can leave me at any time and go live a normal life. You can hit the gay scene and do whatever wild thing your heart screams for you to do. Share the kinky twins. Get fucked in public. Have someone hurt you during sex." A sad smile touched Wulf's lips. "Baby, I just don't think that'll ever be me." He moved closer and stroked Beau's cheek. "I could never share you or hurt you."

Before Beau could stop himself, he rolled his eyes. He took Wulf's hand and headed back toward the Jeep. Beau couldn't stay in this place where Wulf had been hurt. Beau dragged Wulf to the passenger side and opened the door. He motioned Wulf inside. "Get in. I'm driving."

A small smile played on Wulf's lips like Beau humored him, but he climbed inside. Beau circled the vehicle and got behind the wheel. He backed out and retraced Wulf's turns until he found the main road. Beau didn't stop until he pulled back into his driveway. Wulf looked worried now. They hadn't spoken a word on the way home. Beau hadn't bothered to explain himself. Sometimes, words were pointless. Beau had to show Wulf how worried about nothing he was, and they needed to do this tonight before Wulf let this destroy them. Beau headed inside. Wulf followed at a slower pace. The moment Beau stepped through the door, he stripped on his way to the kitchen. Wulf silently stayed on his heels.

While completely nude, Beau snagged a bottle of chocolate syrup from the cabinet. It hadn't been opened yet, so he worked on that.

"Take off your clothes."

Wulf didn't argue. He immediately began removing his clothes at Beau's demand. The moment Wulf took off his shirt, Beau squirted chocolate syrup onto his nipple. He swooped in and sucked it away. The noise that came from the back of Wulf's throat let Beau know he was on the right path.

"Don't stop. I want the rest of those clothes gone."

While he waited for Wulf to lose the pants, he smeared more syrup on Beau's other nipple and sucked.

"Do you like chocolate too? Do you want to get dirty with me? I have some whipped cream too. We could throw an old sheet down and grab my toys. You could eat chocolate and cream from my body while you fuck me, or we could share a double-sided dildo."

"Yes."

Beau hid a triumphant smile. There was no need to gloat. He grabbed a can of whipped cream from the fridge, tucked it under his arm, and then headed for the bedroom with Wulf in tow. After setting their treats on the bedside table, he found the old sheet and covered the bed. Beau waited until he had Wulf on his back covered in gooey sugar with a vibrating butt plug in his ass before he spoke his mind.

He licked a line of chocolate from Wulf's cock. "This is all the kinkiness I need. I don't want to share or for you to hurt me." Beau sucked for a moment, keeping Wulf hard and distracted before going back to his gentle lecture. "I don't know what made you think kink meant pain or humiliation. It can be soft and personal as hell."

Beau slithered up Wulf's body and slid a milking masturbating toy over Wulf's leaking cock. It was double-barreled. Beau slid his dick inside the second slot and hit the button. A gasp tore from his throat as it sucked and massaged. He touched his lips to Wulf's ear to teach him another amazing kink: praise. "That's it. You're such a good and beautiful boy. I knew the first time I let you inside you would be amazing.

You're beautiful inside and out. I want to be with you forever. This is what a good life looks like. A real life. This is what life with me will always be like." A ragged breath tore from Beau as the toy pumped him closer to the edge much faster than he wanted to go. He had been playing with Beau's body and it fucked with him. He was too aroused to hold back much longer. "You're all the kink I need. I don't want bad things. I want good things. Good like you. You're good. No other voice exists but mine. Do you understand? This is a happy place with me. Only happy things happen here."

Wulf stared at him and gasped for air. He looked desperate and ready to cry. Wulf looked vulnerable as he came. "I love you."

Beau ended up being the one who cried as his body jerked with release. His sweet angel needed saving. He needed

Beau's love. Wulf was every bit as perfect as Beau claimed. Beau intended to shelter that and give him peace. That meant getting to the bottom of Wulf's secret life. It was time he found out everything Wulf kept hidden from him. It was time for Beau to learn what Wulf really did for a living.

Chapter Four

WULF'S PHONE DINGED.

Beau kept his eyes shut and his breathing even as Wulf rolled from the bed. Wulf headed for the bathroom. While the water ran, Beau slipped from the bed and pulled on a pair of workout shorts and quickly jumped beneath the covers again. When Wulf stepped out from the bathroom again, Beau feigned sleep. Since Wulf's revelations about his past a month ago, Beau had started asking more questions about Wulf's work.

HAZARDOUS

Before that conversation, Beau hadn't realized how much Wulf kept from him, or how important it was that he knew it all. Wulf wasn't the type to talk about things, and Beau didn't know how to force him. Beau wasn't dumb. He knew damn well Wulf wasn't making all that bank cleaning up crime scenes. If Wulf wouldn't tell him anything willingly, then crazy schemes it was. He was left with no other choice but to find out the truth for himself.

Wulf sat on the edge of the bed. "Hey, angel. Sorry to wake you, but I have to go to work."

Beau pretended to wake. "Oh. Okay." He glanced at the clock. "Be careful. It's the witching hour."

A smile exploded across Wulf's face. "You're so weird."

"That's why you love me."

Wulf didn't stop smiling. "Probably. I do love you, though. Go back to sleep. I'll see you tonight."

Beau nodded, as if he was already halfway there, when, in reality, he plotted. "I love you too." They shared a sweet kiss before Wulf left. Beau wasted no time following.

At sixteen, he had sneaked from his house every weekend and had never been caught. It had been easy because no one suspected him. Maybe someone should have. Then maybe he wouldn't have ruined his life. Tonight felt like the same. The roads were dead in their small town. Beau kept his headlights off and his distance. He had no problem tailing Wulf. With each mile, he prayed he wasn't about to learn something horrible. Something he couldn't unlearn. When they reached the boat docks, following Wulf became even easier. Beau knew the place like the back of his hand. This was where he had met Tim and Wayne each weekend as a teen. Bad memories crowded his brain, making him volatile tonight.

He parked in an alley and followed on foot. Unfortunately, he got there just in time to see it all. Wulf moved from person to person, pulling the trigger. Flashes of light lit the night sky. If Wulf showed any emotion at all, Beau couldn't tell through the biohazard gear. This job of Wulf's was so much worse than anything Beau imagined, and he had no clue how to approach this. With his heart in his throat and his pulse pounding in his ears, Beau made his way back to his truck. For much longer than necessary, he sat in the dark and stared at nothing. No genuine thoughts floated to the surface to save him from himself. In fact, he wondered what it said about him he felt no different about Wulf than he had before he left the house. Probably nothing good. Definitely nothing he hadn't already known before tonight. For certain, something he hadn't wanted to accept. Beau was everything this town thought he was: rotten to his core. He gave no fucks Wulf was a cold-blooded murderer. In fact, he would bet good money Wulf had a good reason. Damn. It didn't even matter if he did. Beau loved him anyhow.

One thing Wulf had never and probably would never adjust to was getting dragged out of bed in the middle of the night and then working all night. It felt unnatural to sleep during the day. That was why he always made himself stay awake all day too, so he could go to bed with Beau. Unfortunately, there was no guarantee he wouldn't get called to work again the next night, and his ass was dragging today.

As he pulled into the driveway at noon, after nine hours of working, Wulf went from thinking he might fall out from the exhaustion to wide awake at the sight of Beau's truck in the driveway. It was funny how Beau made everything better. He was like a shot of adrenaline every damn day, even when Wulf wasn't expecting him.

Beau was asleep on the couch. Wulf closed the front door and crossed the room, hoping not to wake him. He tried to be as quiet as possible while emptying his pockets. Wulf didn't want to disturb Beau until he was ready. He peeled off his shirt and crawled onto the couch with Beau.

"Mhmm."

Wulf smiled at the tired-sounding hum Beau made as he accepted Wulf's weight, half crushing him as Wulf snuggled in with him. He grabbed a nearby throw blanket and covered them.

Beau kissed the tip of Wulf's nose.

Wulf wanted to let him sleep, but he was too curious. "You didn't go to work today."

"I wanted to be here to take care of you when you got home."

Fuck. He didn't stand a chance against Beau. When a person had had no one care about them their entire life, then someone like Beau came along. It was fucking surreal. It was addictive. He would kill to keep this. Honestly, it scared him shitless to think about what he might do to hang on to Beau. Wulf snuggled closer.

"How did everything go last night?"

Wulf kissed Beau's neck. "The same as always. Exhausting. Is it okay if we just sleep for a while? I just want to hold you and try to get a few hours of sleep before they call me in again."

"Of course, baby." Beau tucked them in tighter and wrapped his arms around Wulf. Wulf pressed his ear against Beau's chest. He listened to the sound of Beau's heart beating while his eyelids got heavier by the second.

As sleep tried sucking him under, Wulf couldn't stop himself from baring his heart. "I'm pretty sure you're the only thing keeping me alive. I don't remember why I bothered before you." The confession was forgotten the moment

the darkness swallowed him, but that
didn't make it any less true.

Chapter Five

BEAU SKIMMED HARDY AND Hale's pool while he watched the pair on the sly. They were a bit more subdued than usual today, lingering in the water at the opposite end of the pool from where Beau worked. Unlike usual, they hadn't asked him to take off his shirt. Maybe it was him. He hadn't invited conversation. Beau had been lost in his thoughts. But they too seemed wrapped up in something, and Beau couldn't stop looking their way. They kissed several times without shame. Beau knew a lot of peo-

85

ple would be bothered by them. He knew enough of their story and their life that he wasn't. Even if he hadn't known their history, Beau had never been bothered by them because what the fuck ever. He didn't have to live their lives or be in their heads. Why should he care? Something about the uphill battle they had chosen spoke to him today. Beau felt like they held some wisdom he needed.

"I'm pretty sure you're the only thing keeping me alive. I don't remember why I bothered before you."

Beau couldn't stop thinking about that confession or what he had seen when he followed Wulf to work three nights ago. He had always suspected Wulf was a criminal, which meant his brother-in-law was too. Honestly, after much soul searching, Beau believed this was something he could live with, as long as Marshall knew too. The problem was, as much veiled questioning as he had done without luck, he didn't think he would get anywhere if he asked Wulf point blank. That meant he might have to do something a little crazy. His gaze slid Hardy and Hale's way again. He felt like that was something they would understand, and he needed advice.

Beau set his skimmer aside and moved to their end of the pool. When the pair looked up, Beau dropped to his ass and sat next to them. "Is it okay if I ask you two something deeply personal? You don't have to give detailed answers. Just yes or no answers will suffice."

"Sure," Hale answered for the both of them.

Beau nodded and jumped in with both feet. "Was there a specific event that made you decide you no longer cared what society said was right and wrong? Was there a moment where you said fuck this invisible line in the sand? I want what I want."

"Yes." They both answered so fast, there could be no doubt they both knew exactly when it happened.

Beau took a breath. Even to his ears, it sounded ragged. "I know I said yes or no questions only, but can you tell me if it was something big or something small?" Because honestly, Beau couldn't tell the difference any longer. He only knew he wanted to be with Wulf, and he couldn't tell any longer if reality mattered.

"For me, it was something big," Hale said.

"For me, it was something small." At Hardy's answer, Beau's confusion doubled. He had thought the pair had the same memory or event in mind, but if they hadn't been driven to the extreme by the same monumental moment, then maybe learning his man was a full-blown criminal wasn't his moment to cross all lines in his life.

Hardy touched Beau's knee, pulling him from his roiling thoughts. "If you're questioning if you should cross a line that you know is keeping you from the ultimate happiness, then you already know the answer. Fuck that line, because most of the time, we're the ones drawing it and it's all bullshit anyhow."

Beau felt dejected as hell. He didn't know if he could be who Wulf needed, because he had already gone to jail for one man. But Beau was so, so in love with Wulf, and Beau hadn't stopped thinking about that stupid doghouse. Wulf deserved peace. From what he had witnessed the past three nights of following Wulf to work, Beau honestly didn't believe Wulf was getting any rest in his spirit. He needed someone to show up and out on his behalf. Beau was that person.

Hale took his hand.

Beau's gaze moved to hold the aqua blue stare that nearly matched the pool's water. "Babe, you're a complete badass. You can have and do anything you want. Why do you think we like you so much? The morally gray can always spot their equal. Whatever you're planning to do, you can do it... unless it's murder. I wouldn't advise that."

"Unless they deserved it," Hardy added, surprising a laugh from Beau. "Either way, we'll still love you."

He genuinely cared for these men. They were more than his clients. Beau considered them friends. He hoped Wulf felt the same someday because he had the feeling not only did Hale and Hardy need some real friends, so too did Wulf.

Something seemed off about Beau tonight, but Wulf couldn't put his finger on it. Since Beau walked through the door, he had been unusually subdued. He had stopped to smell the lilies Wulf had bought him several times, but he hadn't spoken much. Wulf caught him staring into space a few times, as if forgetting what he was doing. Around the tenth time, Wulf couldn't take it any longer.

"Did your day go okay? It's Wednesday. Let's see. That's kinky twins day, right?"

A bright smile snapped to Beau's lips. He snorted. "Yes." He rolled his eyes.

"I wish you'd stop calling them that. They're actually really nice. I think you'd like them. It's not their fault they spent their formulative years being fetishized by everyone, and then when they wanted money for what everyone expected of them, they were made pariahs."

Honestly, when Beau put it like that, that was fair.

Beau didn't stop there, really getting heated. "A lot of people are doing morally gray things just trying to survive life: smoking weed, giving blow jobs in public, and punching Nazis. This world is too judgmental. Let people be happy and maybe punch bad people in the dick when no one is looking."

Wulf couldn't stop smiling at Beau's adorable outrage. He was definitely in a mood tonight. "You're really pretty perfect, you know that, right?"

Beau pulled an odd face. "I'm really not. Not at all."

Wulf's face screwed up in confusion. It wasn't the first time Beau had said something along those lines, and he never understood why Beau felt like that. They had been together damn near a year and Beau never failed him. Plus, under normal circumstances, Beau had enough confidence for three people, yet he still pretended he was a bad person sometimes. He wasn't. Wulf knew bad people. He dealt with them daily. His phone dinged, as if proving his point. Wulf growled and grabbed the device. As always, it was only an address.

Beau eyed his phone, reading over his shoulder. "Time to go to work, huh?"

Wulf didn't try to hide it from him. "Unfortunately." Wulf tackled Beau, flattening him on the couch. Beau roared with laughter as Wulf kissed every place he could reach. "Nom. Nom. I miss you already."

Beau shoved at his chest. "Yeah. Yeah. Go do your job. The quicker you leave, the faster you can come back to me."

Wulf didn't budge. He sank into Beau and covered Beau's mouth with his. Their tongues met and stroked. He heard Beau's breath catch. Wulf's cock stirred at the sound. "Fuck. I don't want to go."

"Then stay," Beau said, sounding like a siren luring him to his demise. "I can support us. Just quit. I'll take care of us, and you can actually get some sleep at night."

Wulf pretended to cry. He had never been more tempted by anyone or anything, but sometimes working was about more than making money. "I can't do that, baby." He pressed his forehead against Beau's and stared into Beau's eyes. "I need this job, so I can always spoil you the way you deserve. Say you understand."

"I understand." Beau sounded too solemn, as if he saw too much.

Wulf stole another kiss and pushed himself from the couch. "I love you. I'll text you when I get home, so you'll know I made it safely."

Beau rolled to his side and watched Wulf gather his things. "Okay. I love you too. Be careful."

He was oddly more reluctant to leave tonight than usual. Something still didn't feel right. There was a sense of dread in Wulf's gut as he made his way to the address on his phone. Even as he swapped vehicles and geared up, Wulf stayed inside his head. He didn't speak to anyone as he turned over every moment of his night with Beau. What was different? What was wrong? Wulf screwed on his silencer and moved toward the two bodies and shot each one in the head.

"Did you just shoot those dead men in the head?"

Wulf jumped so hard, he pulled a muscle in his back as he spun at the sound of Beau's voice. Beau stood at the edge of the bloody scene, looking like a babe lost in the woods.

"Yeah, apparently, that's a thing he does now," Jericho said, sounding completely unmoved, as if Beau showed up every night, and this wasn't the most fucked-up thing to happen to him in years.

Dante groaned. "Marshall is going to fucking kill us all."

While—stupidly—trying to hide his weapon, Wulf stepped over a body and moved Beau's way. "Baby, you can't be here."

Beau looked unconcerned by his panic. "I'm pretty sure you can't shoot dead bodies, but you just did, so my being here seems like small potatoes at this point. So why can't I be here?"

He couldn't believe this was happening. Beau was so damn calm. He had to get Beau out of here.

Ender stepped from the shadows with a high-powered rifle pointed at Beau's head. "Hands up."

"That's why you can't be here," Wulf said, sounding weak even to his ears. He wondered if he would faint.

"Yep. Dead. Marshall will see us all stone-cold dead."

Wulf's eyes fell closed. He didn't doubt Dante's words for a second, but first, they had to hope Zander didn't kill them. Honestly, it was just a race at this point.

Truth be told, Beau had always been a little crazy. He didn't know how he had kept it hidden from Wulf for a full year. In his defense, he had a much rougher life than anyone knew. Beau had never been good at thinking things all the way through. Honestly, that was the real reason why he had only ever worked for his brother and stayed on a short leash. Now that he sat inside his living room with a gun pointed at his head, it seemed super short-sighted for him not to have expected to have ended up here. He was an idiot, after all. Since worse things had happened to Beau in his life and Wulf sat by his side, he wasn't nearly as scared as he should have been. Plus, it was strangely satisfying to know he had caught Wulf unawares and Wulf couldn't lie his way out of this. Secrets had cost Beau everything once before in his life. Never again. Wulf kept casting him worried glances. Some ungodly hot dude held the gun to his head, and no one spoke. They all just sat together and waited. For what, Beau didn't know, but he had kicked his way right through that invisible line in the sand. Yep. He had kicked that line's ass. Beau might die for it. He somehow doubted it, though, because his brother-in-law was there, and Marshall would tear this town apart if anyone hurt him. Beau doubted Wulf would appreciate having his home burned to the ground. Countless weird thoughts ran through Beau's head in his attempt at staying calm. It was funny what staring at death looked like. Lots of thoughts bombarded him.

Finally, the front door opened. Everyone shifted slightly. A group of three men poured in. They were huge. Beau found the fear he had been hiding from and he didn't like it. There was something in these men's eyes that had been missing in everyone else's in the room. Or maybe there was something missing from these men's eyes that everyone else in the room possessed and—for the first time—Beau realized how much trouble he was in.

The guy in the middle, and the smallest of the three, seemed to be the one in charge. His long blond hair was perfectly brushed, and his suit looked expensive. He sat while the massive men with him flanked him, taking up protective positions, which humored Beau when it absolutely shouldn't have, but really. He didn't understand what anyone thought he could do. In fact, they held a gun on him. It was the middle of the night, and he was exhausted. Maybe delirium had set in.

The blond tapped a file on his knee and stared at Beau with empty eyes. Beau realized they had met once before. It had only been briefly. At Marshall and Dante's wedding. His name was Zander. Beau only recalled that much because he had gone to high school with a guy with the same name and—oddly—they kind of looked alike, even though Zander was probably fifteen to twenty years older than Beau. Otherwise, Beau had been fully focused on Wulf that day.

Zander was fully focused on Beau today. It was unpleasant. "Well, we have quite a conundrum here, don't we?"

"I don't, since I have no idea what's going on, but you seem to, so…"

Dante covered his eyes as if he couldn't believe Beau's audacity.

Wulf touched his knee. "Baby."

Beau jerked away. "Don't 'baby' me. This is my house. That dude is holding a gun on me, and everyone is acting like I'm wrong. Fuck that."

Zander gestured for the guy with the gun to lower his weapon. He did as told. Zander's eerie-looking eyes moved back to Beau. "Wulf works for me."

"Okay."

Wulf squeezed his knee again, as if trying to get him to be quiet. Beau just wasn't capable for some reason.

Zander kept talking as if he didn't hear Beau's defiance. "It's my job to ensure my employees are kept safe on and off the job, so—once again—we have quite a conundrum here."

Dante jumped in, surprising Beau. "I don't understand the real issue here. Beau is Marshall's brother. Marshall knows about us, and Beau and Wulf have been dating for like a year now. It seems inevitable he be brought into the fold. Unless you're not serious about him," Dante added, looking Wulf's way.

Wulf lunged on the topic, as if he too saw a way to salvage whatever was happening. "Exactly. We're in love. Beau and I practically live together already.

The only reason I haven't told him everything about my job is because I haven't okayed it with you. But now that you're here, and he obviously isn't totally in the dark, and he isn't flipping out, this seems like a good time."

Now they were getting somewhere. Beau was finally about to find out what Wulf had been keeping from him. This unspoken thing that had been stopping them from moving to the next level was about to be gone. He was finally about to see behind the curtain.

Zander tapped the file on his knee again. His gaze moved Beau's way. Ice filled Beau's veins. "No."

"What?" Wulf sounded confused and hurt.

Beau blinked, and a terrible sense of dread overcame him. He had only felt this way once before in his life, but he recognized it immediately. Zander had judged him and ruled against him with no care for the truth.

"I'd like you all to leave now." Beau didn't know why he said the words or where they came from. He just opened his mouth and his heart spoke, because his soul already knew.

Zander opened the file. "How much does Wulf know about you, Beau?"

A pit opened in Beau's stomach. The backs of his eyes burned. His lungs were on fire. "Stop. You've made your point."

"No. We're just getting started."

Beau wondered if he would puke. "You've won. I get it. You don't want me. Now get out."

He felt Wulf's stare and Zander didn't stop. "Does Wulf know you were arrested at sixteen for sexual assault and served two years in a juvenile detention center?" Wulf withdrew his hand from Beau's knee and Zander kept talking. "I mean, I know he had you investigated, but these records were sealed. Before I had them unsealed, that is."

Beau shot to his feet. "Get the fuck out of my house."

Zander stood. "Gladly."

Beau couldn't breathe. He couldn't look at anyone. It was like he was sixteen all over again and couldn't defend himself. He was sixteen again, and no one believed him. Then he was alone in his living room and Beau forced himself to look around. Wulf hadn't stayed. Neither had Dante, and Beau remembered why he had never cared about anyone before Wulf. Not even his own brother, really. Not completely. Because no one believed he wasn't a monster, not really.

Not even him, and that was the scariest shit of all.

Zander stayed at Wulf's place, crowding his space and his peace. He sent Pytor and Yaro to a hotel, but Zander wouldn't go away. Wulf knew Zander was worried about his mental health. He couldn't think straight enough to hang on to a single destructive thought. Wulf couldn't stop picturing Beau's face and thinking it couldn't be true. Zander assured him it was and even showed him Beau's sealed records. According to Beau's file, he had been caught in the act of sexually assaulting a fifteen-year-old boy when he had been sixteen. In exchange for pleading guilty, he had been given two years in a juvenile facility and ordered to complete a sexual rehabilitation program. His records had been sealed upon completion of his sentence. Wulf felt sick and torn. When he had investigated Beau, he had known Beau had a juvenile record, but he hadn't expected anything serious. He loved Beau. The feeling wouldn't go away. He couldn't kill his emotions, but he had fallen in love with a rapist and his stomach felt queasy. It was like being violated all over again.

When a knock landed on the front door, Wulf couldn't bring himself to answer. He didn't care if he ever moved again. His mind was on lockdown. Thankfully, Zander had no qualms about answering someone else's front door. Marshall stepped inside. He didn't look at anyone as he crossed the room and set a large cardboard box on the coffee table with a thump.

"What's this?"

Marshall still didn't look his way. "It's every gift you gave Beau."

"Oh. Thanks." Wulf didn't know what else to say. He hadn't expected Beau to return anything.

Marshall snorted and headed back toward the still open door.

Zander stopped him. "I just want you to know I'm sorry about what happened, and I don't hold family against anyone. I know no one gets to choose their relations."

"Go fuck yourself."

Wulf blinked.

Zander did too. "I'm sorry."

Marshall didn't heed the bite in Zander's tone. "I know you are, and I stand by my statement." He looked Wulf's way. "And that goes for you too. Go fuck yourselves. None of you deserve my brother."

"Your brother is a rapist."

Marshall slammed the door and turned to face Zander at Zander's remark. He hovered over Zander by a good seven inches. "I suggest you take that back."

"I suggest you remember who you're speaking to. We're alone here and I'd hate to hurt Dante by making you disappear."

Marshall ran his tongue across his teeth like he relished the fight. "Oh, I disagree. I'd say you should recognize you're trapped in here with me. Maybe if someone puts their foot in your ass, you'll think twice before spreading lies and ruining someone's life next time."

Wulf shot to his feet and got between them before things went any further. No good would come of any of this. "Let me walk you out."

Marshall walked backward, keeping his gaze locked on Zander. It was obvious he was beyond caring about his safety and someone needed to think straight. Once they were on the porch and Marshall was out of danger of being killed, he turned his ire Wulf's way. "You know, I knew you two were dating, but I stayed quiet because Beau was happy. He was happier and healthier with you than I'd seen him in a long time. I figured you two would come clean about your bullshit when you were ready." Marshall blinked rapidly, as if fighting back his emotions. "Fuck y'all for giving him hope that good people exist." The pain in Marshall's voice spoke to something inside Wulf and broke through in a way nothing else had.

He watched Marshall walk to his truck and his brain seemed to finally start clicking inside his head again. Since the day he met Beau, there had been something about them as a couple—like they were two fake people trying to build a real life. Yet their love had been real. They had fallen in love with half-truths, but Wulf knew Beau. He had seen Beau's face. Heard his plea for Zander to stop talking. That desperation... Wulf recognized that exact desperation.

Without even his shoes, Wulf headed for his Jeep. He drove to Beau's with his heart in his throat. Why hadn't he seen Beau for who he was before now? Holy shit. He felt absolutely sick. Wulf pulled to the side of the road when his stomach heaved. Even with no food on his stomach, he dry heaved for several minutes.

He didn't know the details. Wulf didn't have to know, because he recognized the look in Beau's eyes. He knew the screech of pleading in Beau's voice because he had made those same sounds before. Everything made perfect fucking sense now. He couldn't get to Beau fast enough. Wulf couldn't try to save him quickly enough. Beau's car wasn't in the driveway. Wulf didn't bother knocking. He used his key to get inside. The entire place had been trashed. Beau's TV was smashed, and the vase of flowers Wulf had given him was in pieces on the living room floor.

With his heart in his throat, Wulf headed for the kitchen. Every dish was broken. Glass covered every surface. It cut into his bare feet. His blood mixed with dried blood that already coated the kitchen. Wulf limped to the bedroom. The dresser drawers were all open and all the clothes were gone. His closet was empty, and the bed was stripped. There were no toiletries in the bathroom. Wulf sat on the bed. Beau was gone and Wulf didn't know how to fix him. After all, he had never known how to fix himself.

Chapter Six

JERICHO SAT WITH HIS cup of hot tea in the corner booth of a tiny tea shop on Main and watched the man read. It was a fantasy book today. Edward Jones was of average height and build. He had brown hair and eyes. There was nothing that stood out about him in any crowd, but Jericho saw no one else because one time he had accidentally bumped into Edward on the sidewalk outside the bookstore. Edward had looked up, and the sun had hit his eyes at just the right angle, making them pop. He had blushed and stammered an apology while gathering the books he dropped. They had bumped heads as Jericho tried to help, and Jericho swore the guy nearly cried in his embarrassment. They hadn't exchanged names. Jericho shouldn't know anything about Edward. Edward Jones, who worked at the local library and drove a fifteen-year-old Camry. The guy had an average life and ordinary job, yet he fascinated the fuck out of Jericho, and Jericho could not stop trying to run into him. He had yet to find a single topic to broach with the guy. Today was the day, though.

With his book in one hand and his tea in the other, Jericho moved to push his way from the booth. He hadn't read his book yet, but he could bullshit his way through anything. With Zander in town, bringing in more teams, Jericho had the day off with no chance of getting called in for once. He couldn't miss his chance. Before he made it from the booth, Zander filled the space across from him.

"We need to talk."

Jericho swallowed a tired sigh. Zander was his boss. Jericho couldn't show his irritation. "What's up?" He kept one eye on Edward, hoping he didn't get away before Zander said what he came to say.

"I made a mistake."

That got Jericho's full attention. "I'm listening."

"Marshall told me to go fuck myself."

Jericho had no words because that was either the bravest or the dumbest thing he had ever heard in his entire life. Thankfully, Zander kept talking and saved Jericho from himself.

"The thing is, he kind of shocked me out of my usual rhythm and made me think. No one defends a guilty man with their life like that. So, I thought maybe I was wrong. It made me look at things again. When I unsealed Beau's juvenile records, I was so fucking furious that I just took them at face value. I mean, he pled guilty, and we've been having this whole bullshit with someone trying to infiltrate our organization. It's got me on edge all the time. I thought he'd done it. But Marshall full-on told me to go fuck myself with his whole chest, and that maybe if he put his foot in my ass, I wouldn't spread lies in the future, and you know you wouldn't just do that for anyone. So, I dug deeper."

Jericho fought the urge to gasp and flop around like an old lady with a fit of vapors. He couldn't believe he'd missed this event, or that Marshall would live to tell anyone about any of it. Jericho cleared his throat, trying to sound un-moved. "What did you learn?"

Zander's eyes fell closed, and he pinched the spot between his eyes. Jericho's stomach dropped. He braced for the worst. Zander blew out a breath and focused on Jericho again. "I had Bear track down the victim. It turns out both Beau and this guy Tim were being groomed by their school's SRO officer. He liked to watch them together and other things, of course, but that night, he wanted to watch Beau have his way with Tim. They got busted and the SRO officer pretended he had found them first. He said he had caught Beau assault-ing Tim. Tim panicked and went along with it. The guy was a cop. Of course no one believed Beau. He pled guilty for a lesser sentence that wouldn't ruin his entire life. Of course, Tim is grown now and has had some counseling and realizes he was young and groomed. Fuck, Jericho. I'm better than this. I've just been spread so fucking thin, and I can only see what's on paper. But that's no excuse, and I ruined people's lives here."

"I'm assuming you told all this to Wulf."

Zander's shoulders fell. "After Marshall showed up to tell us all to get fucked, Wulf disappeared. I'm guessing he saw the same thing in Marshall that I did, but he didn't need the same solid proof as me. He didn't even put on his shoes before tearing out of there. But I'm guessing he didn't find Beau because Corey called saying Wulf showed up there with bloodied feet and babbling about how he should've seen it. He knows what victims look like and he should have seen it in Beau's eyes. So I went to Beau's, and the place was trashed, and there's blood everywhere. Fuck if I know at this point."

Jericho drew a steadying breath. His gaze slid Edward's way. It seemed today wasn't their day after all. He focused on Zander again. "What do you need from me?"

"I need you to help me find Beau. Do you recall Wulf saying anything at all about him that might lead us to where he's gone? Anything at all? I mean, this guy's dropped from the planet. He hasn't used a credit card. No red-light cameras or toll roads have picked up his license plate. He left his house after we did and vanished."

For a moment, Jericho stared at nothing, shaking his head. He honestly didn't know Beau at all. He hadn't made a point of getting to know him. Wulf hadn't acted as if he wanted Beau in their world, so Jericho hadn't pushed. A memory sneaked in of a story Wulf had entertained him with while they worked. "Wait. The kinky twins."

A surprised laugh burst from Zander. "What?"

"The kinky twins," Jericho repeated, getting excited now that he realized he actually did know something about Beau's life. "Beau has these two friends who work in the porn industry. They make a fucking killing because they're twins. Wulf always refers to them as the kinky twins."

"Do you know their names?"

Jericho smiled. "I do."

"Fuck yeah. Let's go."

Jericho grabbed his book and slid from the booth. As he passed Edward's table, he set the book on the edge at Edward's elbow. "Hang on to this for me, will you? I'd like to chat next time I come in." He winked and kept moving without waiting for a response. Jericho would either scare the hell out of his mouse or he had just made the first move. He wasn't sure which yet, but he would find out soon enough.

Wulf stayed with Corey. He couldn't go home and face Zander or the box of gifts that reminded him of Beau. Corey had stitched his feet and given him a sedative, but nothing quieted his mind. He didn't need that box in front of him to picture its contents. Every gift he had ever given Beau had been something meant exactly for him. Now Wulf couldn't understand how he had always seen Beau so clearly without ever seeing him at all. Then again, and once again, Wulf was a failure. He had only ever bothered to look skin deep. That was what he did. Wulf fucked up everything he touched. Every second he spent alone with his mind, the darker his thoughts went. He was good at leveling himself. Wulf excelled at being worthless.

A quick knock at the bedroom door was all the notice he got before Jericho stuck his head inside. "Hey, good. You're awake. We found Beau. Let's go."

Confusion made Wulf slow. "What?" He hadn't known anyone was looking for Beau.

Jericho crossed the room with a pair of soft-looking bunny house shoes. "You can thank Rhett for the shoes. I'll fill you in on the way. Can you walk?"

Wulf sat up and let Jericho slip the ridiculous bright pink slippers over his injured feet. Then he gingerly slid from the bed and hobbled a few steps. "Yeah. I've been making my way back and forth to the bathroom. With these, I'm sure I can get to the car." Now that his mind had cleared a bit, panic swelled. If they were looking for Beau, it couldn't be for a good reason. If they planned to harm him, Wulf had to stop them. "Tell me about Beau. Why have you been looking for him?"

"Because Marshall told Zander to go fuck himself."

Fear nearly swelled Wulf's throat completely closed. He picked up the pace. He had to get to Beau before Zander did. "I know. I was there, but I didn't think that would send Zander after Beau. If Zander is pissed about that, he should punish me."

125

Jericho grabbed his arm, slowing him down. "Take it easy. Lean on me. If you tear open your stitches, it'll take us twice as long to get there." He let Jericho help him outside to a waiting SUV. As they reached the black Hummer, the back door opened and one of Zander's bodyguards stepped out.

Wulf eyed Pytor. His gaze moved past the giant Russian to Zander waiting inside. He wondered if this was to be his final ride. Maybe Zander had decided to punish him after all. Wulf drew a steadying breath. If they thought to hurt Beau, Wulf would willingly be at his side. Wulf climbed inside. It wasn't until they were all crammed inside the SUV and on their way that Zander quietly handed him a file. Wulf didn't look at him. He couldn't. Until he sat with these men who had rescued him as a child, he didn't realize how betrayed he felt by them now. Yes, they had saved him, but they hadn't saved Beau. Wulf didn't know if he could forgive that. He opened the file and read because it was easier than looking at anyone inside the SUV. It took him a second to understand he read a transcript of an interview. Then the words blurred and cleared before blurring again. His throat swelled as he read. Wulf's pulse pounded in his ears and his chest tightened. A tear hit the page. He didn't wipe it away. The more he read, the more Beau made sense. He understood the way Beau hoarded money—like he couldn't depend on anyone in the end, and he was right. Everyone had failed him, especially Wulf.

Wulf closed the file, but he didn't look up. He couldn't. Everything hurt too badly.

"I'm sorry, Wulf. I know that'll never be enough."

Logically, Wulf knew Zander would never victimize a victim. Right then, he couldn't be logical, so he chose to be quiet. When the vehicle stopped outside the twins' house, Wulf wasn't surprised. It made sense Beau would go to them. It made sense they would take him. Wulf climbed out, leaving the file behind. He didn't have a plan. Hell, he didn't know if any of them did. It was possible no one would let them in the door. His biggest fear was Beau was hurt. He hadn't forgotten the trashed house or the blood on the floor, but he had been so upset, he hadn't known where to start looking. His mental health always shut him down when he needed his wits the most. He forgot about his injured feet as he headed for the door. Pytor didn't knock.

He opened the door as if he owned the place.

There were men with cameras and women with snacks. A skinny guy stopped them, looking completely un-ruffled by the presence of five men who looked exactly like the Russian mob.

"Are you here for the shoot?"

"We're here for Beau," Jericho answered for them.

The skinny guy waved them away. "He's out by the pool."

Yaro peeked around the corner. A hum-ming sound came from the back of his throat. "I would very much like to watch this shoot."

The man eyed Yaro. "No free shows."

"I have money."

"Twenty grand."

"Done," Pytor said, obviously trying to make his husband happy.

Wulf didn't give a fuck about any of this. He was already headed for the back door. Jericho and Zander followed. Wulf didn't wait for anyone or permission. The way his heart soared at the sight of Beau in nothing but a skimpy speedo on his stomach on a float in the pool said it all. He would never love anyone else. This was the man for him. Beau had one hand resting on the edge of the pool, keeping him anchored. Even though his face was turned Wulf's way, he didn't react to his presence at all.

Wulf dropped to his haunches at the edge of the pool. He eyed Beau from head to toe. There were several stitched cuts on his arms. They were openly leaking blood. Beau didn't seem to notice or care. "I've been looking for you."

Beau didn't focus on him. He didn't look capable of focusing on anything. "Why? Did y'all have a meeting and decide to kill me after all? You're too late." Beau laughed. It was a weak sound, but it was bitter as hell.

"I love you. I'd never let anyone hurt you."

Beau snorted. "We were built on sand. One wave washed us away." Beau splashed him as he made the claim, pushing his float away in the process. Wulf didn't have pride. No one had ever instilled that in him.

He jumped into the water, house shoes, jeans, and all, and went after Beau's float. He snagged it and held Beau in place.

"Are you high?"

"Are you wearing bunny slippers?"

"Yes."

Beau rolled Wulf's way and then flailed when the float didn't cooperate. Wulf easily caught him. Beau stared up at him with bloodshot and dilated eyes. He took a shuddered breath that tore at Wulf's heart. "I told you; you didn't have to cleave yourself in two to let me in but didn't feel the same about me. I wasn't allowed to exist without my past. You won't be happy until I crack myself open and tell you my momma was never home, and no one ever loved me."

"Stop."

Beau shook his head. "No, because you wouldn't make Zander stop. You had to know my brother was never there. I was always alone. Men are supposed to suck it up and be men with no feelings. But I was lonely when I met Wayne and Tim, and Wayne told me I was pretty. He told me I was special, and he gave me gifts. When things started to turn

132

ugly, he said no one would believe me. That it was his word against mine. Then the worst happened, and he was right." Beau's eyes rolled back in his head, and he took a ragged-sounding breath. It got harder to hear Beau when he spoke. "I believed you. Why couldn't you believe me?"

Real panic had set in about halfway through Beau's story, and Wulf didn't know what to do. "What did you take, Beau?"

"Damn. I'm ready to get home to Legend. These twins are... wow."

Wulf ignored Yaro as he panic-trudged his way toward the stairs. He kept his gaze locked on Beau. He could see every labored breath Beau took. "What did you take, Beau?" Wulf could hear his screams, but he couldn't stop. Beau wasn't responding and his every breath seemed weaker and farther apart.

Zander jumped in and helped Wulf carry Beau out.

"Uh, boss. I think I know what he took."

Wulf's head whipped toward where Yaro was stooped nearby. There was an empty bottle of champagne and two open bottles of prescription pills. Yaro turned the bottles upside down, showing they were empty. Wulf's gaze shot to Beau. He swore he saw the moment Beau's heart stopped and then his did too.

Chapter Seven

A FIRE BURNED IN Beau's throat. He swallowed. That didn't help. Grit glued his eyes closed, but he finally managed to pry them open. His bedroom curtains were drawn, but light filtered through, highlighting his bedroom. Beau blinked. He didn't remember going to bed. In fact, the last thing he remembered was doing blow with Hardy and Hale's director in the bathroom and then slipping him two hundred bucks for two bottles of pain pills. Beau hadn't intended to wake up, much less at home. The scent of coffee and toast made his stomach churn. Beau rolled and winced as his arm stuck to the blanket. The stitches in his arm had obviously leaked at some point and the blood dried to the blanket. A growl gathered in Beau's throat. He just didn't want to do this anymore. None of it. Everything was so goddamn tiring. Life's bullshit was always disproportionate to the happiness. The bitterness choked him all hours of the day.

A loud bang and cursing came from the other room, distracting Beau. His gaze shot to the door. The longer he was awake, the more his mind cleared, and the less things made sense. In a fit of rage, Beau had destroyed this place before he left. Now, several things were set to rights that shouldn't have been. His bag of marbles was on the bedside table where they always stayed, except Beau had given those to Marshall to return to Wulf. Beau's gaze moved to the dresser. All the notes Wulf had written him were once again taped to an unbroken mirror. Beau was downright baffled now. He sat up. As he waited for the room to stop spinning, Beau touched his ears. The diamond earrings were back. It was like an odd dream—like maybe he had died after all, except everything hurt, which didn't make sense.

Beau stood. He wore white shorts he didn't recognize. It was just one more thing that didn't make sense. He headed for the living room and found it completely restored. Nothing was broken or out of place. Wulf stood at the kitchen counter, spreading jelly across a piece of toast. Beau quietly sat at the kitchen table and watched.

"Why were you shooting dead bodies?"

Wulf jumped like Beau had screamed against his ear. He juggled the butter knife for a moment before finally setting it on the tray he had been in the middle of putting together. "Fuck. You scared the shit out of me. I didn't hear you get up. I wanted to bring you breakfast in bed."

It hurt Beau's chest how much he loved this man. "If I get back in bed and let you bring me breakfast, will you tell me why you were shooting dead bodies?"

Wulf looked his way. There were dark circles under his eyes. His brown hair was a mess and his tangled curls hung in his eyes. Like always, Beau wanted to snuggle him and tell him everything would be okay, even though Beau wasn't so sure it was true this time. "Yes."

Beau nodded and stood. He went back to bed and waited. With his back against the headboard, he watched as Wulf carried a tray of food through the door. He set the tray across Beau's lap. Beau's stomach heaved, but he tried to hide it. Nothing felt good. There was ice water and black coffee. Beau sipped the water, hoping it would settle his stomach.

"Eat a little toast. You'll feel better."

Beau doubted it, but he tried.

Wulf sat near his feet and watched—like a protective bear, watching its cub. He was twice as intense today, and that was saying a lot.

The toast scraped his raw throat as he swallowed. Beau winced. Wulf looked away. He uncovered Beau's feet and rubbed them while Beau ate, as if he couldn't watch Beau suffer. "It's painful to have your stomach pumped. I've been there. Five times, actually. I take meds now to stabilize my moods, but

I don't have the greatest mental health. When things get too stressful, I shut down. That's why I fuck up so much. My brain slows down and I just don't handle life as well as a normal person."

"That's bullshit. You're amazing."

Wulf stopped massaging Beau's feet at his outburst. His gaze shifted Beau's way. "You're the only one who thinks that." A small smile touched Wulf's lips, and he went back to staring at nothing while rubbing Beau's feet. "Zander runs an operation that rescues kids from sex trafficking. When these men try bringing the kids in through the docks, Zander has them taken out, and the kids re-homed. My team cleans up afterward. The night I showed up here, the first night we were together, I checked everyone's pulse and didn't find anyone alive. I declared everyone dead. Then Dante moved in to work on disposing of the first body. The guy wasn't dead. He shot Dante in the chest." Wulf looked at Beau again. His eyes looked exactly as they had that night. They were haunted. Beau hadn't been capable of turning his back on Wulf that night and he couldn't now. He listened to every word. "Dante almost died because of my mistake. So now I shoot every downed target before cleanup for good measure. No more chances with anyone's lives."

"What about yours?"

Wulf went back to watching his hands. His hair blocked his expression. Beau didn't need to see his face because he already knew. He had known since the night Wulf showed up on his doorstep. This life wasn't for him. He wasn't the guy who shot dead bodies. Wulf was the guy who made toast and bought marbles.

"I shouldn't have left with Zander. I shouldn't have let him keep talking when you begged him to stop." Wulf's voice got more desperate by the second, and Beau grew stronger, because that was who they were. Wulf took care of Beau and Beau shored up Wulf. They were like two incomplete people who clicked together like puzzle pieces.

"Would you like to marry me?"

Wulf's head shot up. He was crying and Beau could barely breathe. Nothing felt good, except Wulf always had.

"We could just be normal. Like a family. You could come to work with me at Marshall's business. God knows, I need the help. We could work together and just... be normal."

"But I left you."

Beau nodded. "I'm a little crazy."

An angry line appeared between Wulf's eyebrows, as if he planned to argue.

Beau shook his head and waved off whatever Beau was getting ready to say. "It's important to know yourself, and I really am. But the day we met, and you showed me how much money is in your bank account, I immediately knew you were just like me. I knew you were a survivor. It was obvious you were out here doing whatever it took to be beholden to no one. Just like me. When you showed up on my doorstep, looking ready to fall apart, it felt like we were meant for each other. But if someone I trusted told me you were a rapist, maybe I would've believed it too. Maybe for a minute. But you're sitting here right now, so you must not think that anymore and that makes you the only person who's ever believed me." Beau's voice broke as he said the words.

"You would never do such a thing." Wulf said the words with such raged-filled confidence that Beau felt vindicated in a way he never had.

Beau held Wulf's stare. "I wouldn't."

"And I'm not the only one who believes in you," Wulf said, sounding ready to march into battle. "Marshall was ready to throw down with Zander, which probably had him closer to getting killed than he realizes. The twins took you in without blinking. Zander replaced everything in your house to apologize for his accusations. You're not alone, but even if none of those people believed, I would. I will always be on your side. I will always have your back. If you ever try to off yourself again, I will kill you myself. You don't get to leave me."

Beau bit his bottom lip. He kind of liked this side of Wulf. Beau stared at Wulf from beneath his lashes and waited for Wulf to catch his breath. Wulf went back to rubbing Beau's feet. Beau went back to nibbling his toast. He didn't want to talk about downing those pills. Beau wasn't ready. He didn't know why he hadn't woken up in a mental institution, but he imagined that was on Zander too. Beau had spent years working on himself only to let this bullshit level him again, and he needed to rebalance himself. He needed normal.

"As it happens, Zander fired me." Wulf sounded calm, as if they talked about the weather. "Well, he called it a mental health evaluation failure or some other such nonsense, but I was given a hefty severance and told I can come back anytime I feel I'm up to the challenge. Obviously, I'm still part of the family." Wulf said that part using air quotes before going back to rubbing Beau's feet. "They'll still be taking care of all my medical needs and whatnot since Zander will still likely have me doing odd jobs here and there. I can't complain. It's not like I'm not already set up for life, but yeah. A normal life sounds good."

"I love you."

Wulf smiled. "I love you too. Sorry for rambling."

Beau shook his head. "There's nothing I'd rather be doing than listening to you ramble." Guilt sideswiped Beau. "How much does Marshall know? I'm always a burden to him."

"Nothing. Zander kept Dante out of things yesterday and everyone else is paid very well to be discreet." For a moment, Wulf stared at Beau in silence. He stroked Beau's leg. "Zander is like us, you know. That's why he reacted so badly to unsealing your file. He didn't know it was a lie. I'm not defending what he did. Like I said, I'm always on your side. I'm just saying Zander understands why you did what you did yesterday, and maybe if you decide you need someone to talk to besides me, then he has the means to set that up."

Beau set his barely touched toast aside. "Why is Zander all the sudden apologetic and on my side?"

"He sent someone to talk to Tim."

Beau flinched. He couldn't help it. That was a name he hadn't heard in years. "I don't feel so good."

Wulf jumped up and moved the tray. "What can I do to help?"

Beau took a breath, but it was like nothing happened. No air reached his brain. He fanned his face.

"Holy shit." Wulf dragged Beau to the edge of the bed and shoved his head between his knees. "Just breathe, baby. It's okay. I'm right here with you."

Beau stared at the floor. It blurred as Wulf stroked his back and spoke to him softly.

"You're just having a panic attack. It happens to me all the time. I know it feels like dry drowning or like a heart attack, but I've got you."

Beau sucked in a deep breath. It sounded painful even to his ears. He thought he had moved past all this years ago. His records had been sealed. He had moved on with his life. Beau worked a grown-up job and lived a responsible life. It had been years since he let the sound of one name completely take the air from his lungs. But Wulf stayed with him, and each breath came easier.

"You know, I would very much like to be married to you," Wulf said as he kept rubbing Beau's back like nothing happened—like Beau wasn't a complete mess. "I know I bitch about your hobbit house vines, but they've grown on me. Or we could buy a different house in the twins' neighborhood, so you could be closer to your friends. I can afford to live wherever you want. We could go to work together every day before coming home together each night. We could take turns having panic attacks and stalking each other. We can only be crazy at the same time occasionally, though. We'll have to take turns at that."

A laugh burst from Beau. He honestly didn't know how he had lived before Wulf. Beau sat up and leaned into

Wulf's hold. He had spent his night at Hardy and Hale's house, coming completely unglued. Years of therapy and hard work had been undone by a single moment. Beau had burst onto Wulf's job site ready to fight to save their relationship from Wulf's job and it turned out he was nowhere near as strong as he thought.

"I so wanted to be your hero."

Wulf held him tighter. "You're better than that. You're my best friend. God, I've needed the love and friendship you've given me so much more than I've ever needed a hero in my life. You're the only real family I've got. If you bail, I've got nothing. I may as well go with you."

Beau sniffed. He felt like absolute shit, physically and mentally. "Do you think you could just hold me for a little while?

I just want to cuddle with you for a while."

"You know you don't need to ask. I need you to drink some water first, though. Corey says you have to clear your kidneys."

Beau nodded and accepted the water Wulf passed his way. He polished off the glass because he loved Wulf and he never wanted to let him down again. After setting the empty glass aside, Wulf moved the tray to the dresser, and they snuggled up together on the bed. Beau let the sound of Wulf's steady heartbeat soothe him. He had let himself have a setback, but it wouldn't happen again. Wulf wanted a normal life. Beau would make sure he got one. Maybe he didn't know how to be sane for himself, but he could do it for Wulf. Beau could do anything for Wulf.

Wulf hadn't truly slept since Beau burst onto his job. Everything had been too big of a mess. It seemed like the minute he settled on his side with Beau cuddled against him, he was out, and he had no clue what day or time it was when his eyes opened again. He was alone. Wulf didn't like that. For a moment, he glared at the darkened ceiling until muted voices reached his ears. His bladder outbid his curiosity for the win. Wulf made a quick trip to the bathroom before going after his man. Beau would explain why he had left Wulf alone in bed. He didn't care who else was there for the explanation.

Beau didn't have a huge house. It was only three bedrooms and two bathrooms, but it was cozy. There weren't many places for Beau to hide. Luckily, Wulf spotted the open back door before he searched too hard. Twinkling lights reflected on the pool water, luring Wulf toward the door. Wulf's steps slowed as voices carried inside the house clearly enough for him to hear.

"Is Wulf planning to sleep all night?"

"I'll go wake him when we finish hanging this strand of fairy lights and Marshall fires up the grill."

Wulf leaned his shoulder against the door frame and peeked out. People didn't usually notice him unless he wanted to be seen. Wulf loved watching Beau when Beau didn't know he was there.

Dante leaned close to one of Beau's lights, inspecting it. "These really do have little fairies inside. That's pretty cool. You have a neat setup here. It's like being inside a fairytale."

Beau flashed Dante a smile. "I always wanted my home to be my personal escape. Reality never suited me much."

Dante nodded and fell silent. He gathered his long blond hair at the nape and pulled it up before dropping it again, looking nervous. "So, hey. Thanks for inviting me tonight. Even though I'm your brother-in-law, I get you didn't have to talk to me again. I shouldn't have left after the shit with Zander, and—if it matters at all—when I got home and Marshall explained your side of things, I actually quit the team. I didn't agree to go back to work until Zander promised he'd make things right with you."

Beau kept his gaze locked on his box of fairy lights. He pulled out a lantern with a fairy inside and lit it. His gaze never moved Dante's way. "If it's all the same to you, I'd rather just forget it. I paid the price to have those records sealed for a reason. All that was supposed to be behind me. I didn't know I was ever going to have to think about it again."

"Are you ready to help me fire up this grill?"

Wulf's heart slammed against his chest as Marshall seemed to materialize at his side from nowhere with a lighter and charcoal. He tried to hide his surprise. "Sure."

Beau's head turned Wulf's way. He visibly brightened, as if a fire lit inside him simply because Wulf was there. "Hey. You're awake."

It was another moment that highlighted how wrong Wulf had been for ever doubting Beau, even for a second. Few people were just genuinely good. Beau was. He loved Wulf when no one else ever had. Wulf felt it every second of the day. "Sorry. I didn't know we had company."

The space between them disappeared. Beau kissed him. "It's okay. They're family. I planned to come get you as soon as I finished setting out all my fairy lights. Oh, I want to show you something before Marshall steals you to help with the grill." Beau took his hand and dragged Wulf back inside and headed for the front door. "Dante called some guy he says you two know, and he stopped by and made some adjustments to the security on the porch." Beau opened the front door and pushed leaves aside on his vines that showed hidden motion sensors and cameras. "Dante said we have to have higher security here now anyhow."

Wulf's heart dropped. "This place is supposed to be your sanctuary."

"It is because you're here with me."

For a moment, they held each other's stare in silence. Wulf wished they were alone. "I missed you when I woke up."

"I got hungry." Beau smiled at his own confession. It slipped away as he added, "and I kind of needed my big brother and I think you kind of need to see that you have one now too."

Until Beau said the words, it hadn't even occurred to Wulf that Marshall and Dante would for real be his family once he married Beau. He blinked. "I have a family." Even he heard the detachment in his voice, as if something so profound could never happen to him in reality.

Beau nodded. A sweet smile touched his lips. "Yeah, you do. He's looking at you."

"Come on, guys. These burgers won't flip themselves. I buy. Y'all fry. That's the deal and I'm starving."

Beau snorted. He nodded toward the back, where Marshall called out for them to join. "We should go. Marshall likes to bitch about paying for everything, but it's also his thing. He's a provider. You'll see. I snatched the check away from him at dinner once and he didn't talk to me for the rest of the night."

Wulf shook his head and followed Beau back to the backyard where they left Marshall and Dante. Smoke already poured from the grill. Wulf took a breath and joined Marshall. Marshall handed him a beer. "I was just telling Beau, before you got up, that I have a fleet of trucks at the shop. If we each picked up one, we could have your stuff moved here in a single weekend. We could definitely get it done faster than a moving company."

"Sounds good." Wulf sipped his beer. He didn't know what to say or how to act. As much as he wanted a family, this was new to him. It would take time. Plus, he didn't know how much Beau had told Marshall. He didn't know if Marshall knew they were getting married or if he only thought they were moving in together. Wulf didn't want to say anything without talking to Beau first.

Marshall glanced behind him. Beau was busy showing Dante how to get to the hidden island behind his pool without getting wet. He lowered his voice, for only Wulf's ears. "Thank you for believing Beau. It's been tough as hell knowing that motherfucker Wayne is still working as an SRO at a middle school a town over, and there is not a damn thing I can do about it. But you believed, and that matters. Beau is better when he's with you." Marshall flipped the burgers, making Wulf smile. It was obvious Marshall was incapable of handing over any real control. Beau was right. Marshall was the provider. The head of the family. It was a strange sort of comfort, like Wulf had somewhere to go if he had a problem.

"Beau says you work for me now."

Wulf nodded. "It would seem so. If that's okay with you anyhow? I have quite a few hazardous waste and chemical certifications... obviously, if it matters."

"I don't doubt it, but don't worry about it. Beau's the manager. If he says you're hired, you're hired. It honestly gives me hope, seeing you give up the whole

Zander thing. Sometimes I wish Dante would."

Wulf couldn't even imagine. If Beau had almost died on the job, he wouldn't go back, or Wulf would be there, hounding his every step. Still, whereas Wulf's mental health suffered from working for Zander, Dante thrived. "For the most part, what Dante does is safe, so I don't think you have to worry. Plus, with Zander bringing in new crews, he won't be working anywhere near as much. He needs it, though. He needs to know he's helping the cause."

"And you?" Marshall asked without looking his way. It was obvious he was trying to learn as much as he could without seeming as if he pried.

Wulf didn't mind being honest. "I think I'm more like Beau. The closer I stay to the trauma, the worse I get. I lived eleven years in chains. Not much has felt like it's changed since then. I need the fairytale house." He didn't know if that made sense to Marshall, but he knew it would to Beau. That was what mattered.

Marshall set his hand on Wulf's shoulder and squeezed. "Then I'd say Beau and you are a match made in heaven." Beau headed their way, smiling. Marshall quickly leaned close to Wulf's ear and spoke. "Let's get together and talk about Christmas sometime soon-ish. I think we should go in together and build one of those crazy treehouses for Beau—like the ones on TV."

Wulf quickly agreed before Beau overheard. As Beau wrapped his arms around Wulf's waist and Dante smacked Marshall's ass, Wulf saw a brighter future than he ever had. Hell, he saw a future for once. He saw Christmas with a tree and his new family. Dante would be his brother for real now. Wulf could take Beau on vacations, and they could start weird new hobbies together. Life had never felt so full of possibilities. It was all because of the amazing man next to him. Wulf stared into the hazel eyes of the gorgeous man who had saved him, and he felt his soul healing. They would have a good life together. A solid one. Wulf only had one last person to kill and then they could rest. He couldn't leave a mess one town over at a middle school, for fuck's sake. That was unacceptable. Wulf kissed the tip of Beau's nose. Their sanity demanded a clean slate.

Chapter Eight

A RED BOX SAT on the bed in their chateau, taunting Beau. Wulf still left him little gifts, but this was different. Not only was this box large, it was also gorgeous. Beau wanted to rip it open, but he also hated to hurt such a beautiful box.

"Open it."

Beau giggled. He heard himself. Even to his ears, he sounded like a kid on Christmas. In fact, it was their wedding night. He understood he stared at his wedding gift, and he should open the damn box. Then again, it was kind of fun letting the excitement build. He had been riding a high all day that wouldn't stop. In a small chapel in The French Riviera, Wulf and Beau had exchanged their vows in front of a handful of friends and family. Zander had footed the bill as yet another form of apology. Marshall still wouldn't speak to him. Beau hadn't decided if that was due to footing the bill or nearly ruining Beau's life. Beau knew Marshall would eventually forgive Zander. Marshall was the nicest person Beau knew. He couldn't hold a grudge forever. Beau wasn't sure anyone could be angry in a place this beautiful. By the end of the night, everyone who came for the wedding would come for their spouses and all would be forgotten. At least, that was the fantasy inside Beau's head. Now he had this box and a sexy husband to hold his attention. Beau didn't know where to start.

"Do I have to open it for you?"

A huff burst from Beau. "Why do you sound like this gift is more for you than me? You should open your gift and let me savor mine."

Wulf's dark eyebrows rose. He looked devilish tonight. Marriage and happiness suited him. "I have a gift?"

"Of course," Beau said, rolling his eyes. He crossed the room and grabbed a small box from his suitcase. Beau had taken great care wrapping Wulf's gift. Wulf always made such a big deal of giving him presents. Beau wanted this wedding gift to be perfect. He handed the box to Wulf.

Wulf's expression, as he stared at the silver-wrapped box, filled Beau's chest with so much pride, he thought he might burst. Beau never tired of the way Wulf looked right now. Wulf tugged the shimmering ribbon and set it aside. Beau held his breath as Wulf lifted the lid. He couldn't look away as Wulf took the leather bracelet cuff from inside. Wulf traced the letters and magical designs burned into the piece.

"Wulf and Beau, forever."

"I know it's silly, but Dante told me about a guy that works with the team who makes these leather pieces, and I think it turned out amazing."

Wulf looked up from his gift. "It's not silly. It's gorgeous. Thank you. It's perfect." He put the cuff on his wrist. "It's your turn now. Open your gift."

Since Beau couldn't wait any longer, he rushed to the bed and grabbed his present. It had some weight to it. "Whoa. What's in this thing?"

A coy smile touched Wulf's lips. "Open it, for fuck's sake."

With a huge grin stretching his lips, Beau tore at the paper and flipped open the box flaps. It took him a moment to realize what he stared at. "It's a fireman's costume."

Wulf nodded as he stripped. "Yep. Didn't you call for a rescue?"

Beau covered his mouth, trying to hide the gigantic grin he wore. He couldn't believe how far Wulf had come. Wulf actually intended to role play with him. He watched as Wulf stepped into the bottom half of the uniform. Shirtless, he pulled up the suspenders and Beau fanned his face. "Thank God. A sexy fireman has come to my aid. I'm burning up over here. Someone spilled some hazardous waste and I'm in danger."

To Wulf's credit, he didn't smile. He stared at Beau with a heated gaze that let Beau know they wouldn't play for long. "You need to strip so I can lick you clean."

"Is that standard procedure?"

Wulf bit his bottom lip and looked Beau up and down before meeting his stare. He crowded Beau's space. "Are you questioning an expert?"

Beau covered Wulf's mouth with his. He couldn't stand another second without tasting his new husband. No one had ever turned him on the way Wulf did. He didn't really need the role playing, but adored that Wulf was willing to try. Beau's clothes disappeared beneath Wulf's expert fingers. He swore he tasted Wulf's love on Wulf's tongue.

169

Then Wulf bit Beau's bottom lip and Beau's feet left the floor. The temperature in the room changed. As much as Beau adored Wulf's willingness with the fireman's costume, he had zero patience tonight. Beau had watched Wulf promise to love and cherish him for the rest of their lives today. He needed to consummate that. Plus, Wulf had never bitten him before. That shit was hotter than any costume.

Ragged breaths filled the air as Wulf took Beau down onto the bed. Wulf's mouth moved down Beau's body, kissing and licking. Wet fingers stretched Beau's asshole. Beau lifted his head and watched as Wulf sucked his dick. Whiskey-colored eyes stared up at him. The world seemed to stop for them. Wulf shifted to his knees and pushed Beau's thighs apart. Beau drew his knees higher, exposing himself for the taking.

Wulf never looked away as he teased Beau's asshole with his crown.

"You took in a stray."

Before Beau had time to process Wulf's words, Wulf surged forward and impaled Beau. Beau sucked in a sharp breath. Wulf fell forward and swallowed the sound. He pulled away and backed out before slamming inside Beau once more.

"Now you're stuck with me."

Beau used every ounce of his strength to roll, pinning Wulf beneath him. He rocked himself on Wulf's cock, taking what he wanted. "No. You're stuck with me. That's okay, though." Beau kissed Wulf's chin. "I have candy and cuddles." He kissed the corner of Wulf's mouth. "I'll love you and keep you safe."

In a flash, Beau found himself beneath Wulf again. Wulf pounded inside him, stealing his breath. All Beau could do was hold on to the headboard and feel as Wulf thrust at the perfect angle, taking him to heaven. Beau floated between closing his eyes to focus on the way Wulf played with his body and keeping his eyes open to enjoy the show. Wulf looked so intense and sexy. Beau wanted to memorize every second. The race to the edge came quicker than Beau expected. He found himself scratching at Wulf's skin and begging for release.

"Please. Don't stop. Yes. Right there." Wulf moved faster and faster. The sound of skin slapping skin mixed with their moans and whines. Beau cried out as his body jerked with release. Cum filled the space between them.

Wulf made a guttural sound that Beau swore must have come from his soul. He cried out against Beau's lips. They kissed even as they fought for air. Sweat coated their skin. Pants burst from them. A happy hum filled Beau's mind as love practically had him coming apart at the seams.

"I'm sorry," Wulf said, between kissing and sounding out of breath.

"Why are you apologizing?"

Wulf rolled to his side and threw his leg over Beau, pinning him to the bed. "I meant to drag things out and savor our wedding night. You just do it for me, I guess. I can't stop myself from falling on you like I haven't had sex in ten years."

Beau couldn't stop smiling. His entire face hurt from it. "Damn. I'd much rather hear that than have any amount of foreplay, plus wow. That was..." Beau tried to catch his breath. "Whoa." They were always good together.

Wulf chuckled against his skin.

"Mhmm." He loved the way it felt when Wulf laughed. "The sound of your happiness is reviving me. I might not need the fire department after all."

Wulf laughed harder.

Beau turned his head and met Wulf's stare. He couldn't believe this sexy and perfect man belonged to him now. "You really married me." His throat tightened on the words.

Wulf's features softened. He stroked Beau's cheek. "Once upon a time, there was a wolf under an evil man's curse."

In an instant, Beau's eyes filled with tears.

Wulf didn't stop. "He was starving and beaten, but he spotted this fairy house where a sexy prince took him in."

"It turns out he wasn't cursed at all," Beau interjected, refusing to let Wulf continue. "And it was the prince who needed saving."

Wulf's gaze moved over Beau's face. Beau felt more than saw him shrug. "I'm not sure it matters which version is true. Both stories end the same."

"Happily ever after?"

Wulf rolled and straddled Beau's body. "The prince got eaten by the wolf, but yeah. Then they lived happily ever after."

A laugh burst from Beau. His body shook with it, and happiness radiated from his soul. He knew they weren't the type of people who would ever get to stop working on their mental health, but damned if they wouldn't work harder for each other than anyone else alive. They each understood hell and they would never let the other go there again. This was their safe space. Their happy home. A fairytale life. They would die for this. In some small way, they already had. Now it was Wulf and Beau forever. It didn't matter which of them saved the other first. Either way, a curse had been lifted and they got their happy ending.

Two things, keep an eye out for the next book in the Kings of the East series, *Average*.

Also, if you're interested in reading Hale and Hardy's book, it is called *Mirror Image* and is only available on Smashwords. It's not a book that'll be for everyone, and if you'd like to buy it, you'll have to make sure you have your sensitivity filter turned off to find it. That's located in the upper right-hand corner on the website. It says, "filtering." Click that and choose your settings. If the link doesn't work or the book doesn't show up in search, that's why. Once you turn off that filter, you shouldn't have a problem. Here's the l i n k : https://www.smashwords.com/books/view/1168965?ref=authorCharityParkerson

Please consider leaving a review at the retailer where you purchased this book. Reviews really help with a book's visibility, which allows me to continue writing more stories. Thank you, Charity.

About the Author

CHARITY PARKERSON IS AN award-winning and multi-published author with several companies. Born with no filter from her brain to her mouth, she decided to take this odd quirk and insert it in her characters.

*Eight-time Readers' Favorite Award Winner
*2015 Passionate Plume Award Finalist
*2013 Reviewers' Choice Award Winner
*2012 ARRA Finalist for Favorite Paranormal Romance

*Five-time winner of The Mistress of the Darkpath

Connect with her online:

*Sign up for her newsletter: https://sendfox.com/charityparkerson
*Join her readers' group on Facebook: http://bit.ly/CharitysTribe
*Website: https://www.charityparkerson.com
*A list of her social media accounts and giveaways all in one place: http://hy.page/charityparkerson

Content

CONTENT WARNING: THIS SERIES is darker than my usual writing. Since these books bring back Zander and his fight against child trafficking, the deal in kidnapping, sex trafficking (along with everything entailed in that), suicide, and murder. A lot of these characters survived the worst things imaginable and now live with the scars. But now they fight to save people like them.

www.ingramcontent.com/pod-product-compliance
Lightning Source LLC
Chambersburg PA
CBHW060221180626
46813CB00007B/2917